THE VICIOUS CIRCLE

THE VICIOUS CIRCLE

Mysteries and Crime Stories from the Algonquin Round Table

EDITED BY OTTO PENZLER

FALL RIVER PRESS

This 2009 edition published by Fall River Press,
by arrangement with Pegasus Books.

Fall River Press
122 Fifth Avenue
New York, NY 10011

ISBN: 978-1-4351-1114-1

Printed and bound in the United States of America

1 3 5 7 9 10 8 6 4 2

The pages of this book contain 30% recycled fiber

For Joyce Carol Oates
With respect,
With admiration,
but mostly—With love

Permissions

Introduction © 2007 by Otto Penzler.

Compilation © 2007 by Otto Penzler.

"The Mystery of the Poisoned Kipper" © 1932 by Robert Benchley; renewed 1959. Reprinted by kind permission of The Estate of Robert Benchley; Nathaniel Benchley, proprietor.

"Coroner's Inquest" © 1930 by Marc Connelly; renewed 1957. Reprinted by kind permission of The Dramatists Guild Fund, Inc.

"The Man Who Came Back" © 1911 by Edna Ferber; renewed 1938. Reprinted by kind permission of The Estate of Edna Ferber.

"The Great Warburton Mystery" © by George S. Kaufman and Howard Dietz, 1931; renewed 1958. Reprinted by kind permission of Anne Kaufman Schneider and The Estate of Howard Dietz.

"Haircut" © 1925 by Ring Lardner; renewed 1952. Reprinted by kind permission of The Estate of Ring Lardner.

"Stop Me If You've Heard This One" © 1929 by Ring Lardner; renewed 1956. Reprinted by kind permission of The Estate of Ring Lardner.

"Big Blonde" © 1929 by Dorothy Parker; renewed 1957. From *The Portable Dorothy Parker,* edited by Marion Meade. Reprinted by kind permission of Viking Penguin, a division of Penguin Group (USA), Inc.

"Farewell, My Lovely Appetizer" © 1944 by S. J. Perelman; renewed 1971. Reprinted by kind permission of Harold Ober Associates Incorporated.

"Up the Close and Down the Stair" © 1951 by S. J. Perelman; renewed 1978. Reprinted by kind permission of Harold Ober Associates Incorporated.

"Four-and-Twenty Blackjacks" © 1971 by S. J. Perelman; renewed 1998. Reprinted by kind permission of Harold Ober Associates Incorporated.

Contents

Introduction

HAS THERE EVER BEEN a more exciting decade in the past century than the 1920s—especially in New York? Jack Dempsey lived and fought here, Babe Ruth hit home runs for the Yankees, flappers and their beaus filled speakeasies, Helen Hayes was on Broadway, the Rockefellers, Vanderbilts, Morgans, and Astors dominated the social scene, and the most famous literary coterie in the history of America, the Algonquin Round Table, created itself.

It had not been planned. Writers and editors for *The New Yorker* drifted into the Oak Room of the nearby hotel late in 1919. Since they were well-known and influential, actors and publicists soon followed, hoping for mention in that young but already important magazine. Producers turned up next. The table hopping became so ubiquitous that the hotel manager prepared a very large table in the adjoining Rose Room so that the ever-expanding group could simply be proximate, rather than having to stand around various tables, blocking the aisles to the inevitable irritation of the waiters and the excluded diners.

The big round table was soon full not only at lunch, but at cocktail hour (which lasted for most of the day for many members), dinner, and late night supper as well. It was an amorphous group, informal, and with an ever-changing membership so volatile that it is difficult even to determine who was, in fact, a member.

Dorothy Parker, probably the one person most famously identified as the central figure at the Round Table, in later years denied that she was ever part of it, in spite of the photographs and newspaper and magazine stories and columns of the day in which she was relentlessly quoted. Ring Lardner did not attend the lunches but socialized with numerous members, played poker with them, and wrote skits for a lavish Broadway production, *The 49ers,* that failed because it had so many inside jokes that it was understood by no one besides Round Tablers. Alexander Woollcott, the heart of the group, was among the first to be a regular and among the last to drift away. Harpo Marx was often at the table, as were the columnists Franklin P. Adams and Heywood Broun and his wife, Ruth Hale. The playwrights Marc Connelly, George S. Kaufman, Edna Ferber, and Robert Sherwood were regulars for a while, often meeting to collaborate on new works. The critic and humorous writer and actor Robert Benchley was a mainstay of the group, as was Harold Ross, the founder of *The New Yorker.* Among the many celebrities who often stopped by were Tallulah Bankhead and Noël Coward.

The primary activity of these notables, apart from the consumption of vast quantities of alcohol, seems to have been the display of wit, most of it caustic, often aimed at other members of the group, and just as often at themselves. Woollcott, described by a critic as "the worst writer in America," retorted, "I'm potentially the best writer in America, but I never had anything to say." Benchley, who regarded himself a failure, said, "It took me fifteen years to discover that I had no talent for writing, but I couldn't give it up because by that time I was too famous."

No one in what became known as "The Vicious Circle" was immune from becoming a target for someone else's nasty humor.

After Woollcott autographed a copy of his book *Shouts and Murmurs,* he asked with satisfaction, "Ah, what is so rare as a Woollcott first edition." Adams replied, "A Woollcott second edition."

Woollcott once described his luncheon companion of many years, Harold Ross, as looking "like a dishonest Abe Lincoln." In her youth, Dorothy Parker's vitriolic wit was masked by her look of demure innocence, giving rise to Woollcott's description: "Dorothy Parker is a combination of Little Nell and Lady Macbeth."

When Adams wrote a scathing review of a book by Broun, his fellow Round Tabler Woollcott said, "You can see Frank's scratches on Heywood's back yet."

Edna Ferber, planning a European vacation, said she wanted to be alone on the trip. "I don't expect to talk to a man or a woman—just Aleck Woollcott." On a different occasion, Ferber showed up for lunch at the Round Table wearing one of her tailored suits. Noël Coward greeted her by saying, "You look almost like a man." Ferber replied, "So do you."

Upon the publication of a newly discovered Charles Dickens manuscript, Kaufman, known for his intense work habits, said of Connelly, his former collaborator, just as famous for his casual attitude to work, "Charles Dickens, dead, writes more than Marc Connelly alive."

In the early days of the Round Table, before the petty jealousies and personality frictions eroded friendships, the members were young, talented, and, mostly, struggling to earn money. They hoped to use each other, and also to help each other achieve success, both critical and financial. They accomplished this to a degree, though it has often been noted that virtually none of them ever achieved the heights to which they seemed destined, their names largely lost to history.

Ring Lardner, the greatest of them, was already successful when he befriended members of the group. During the years in which he was closely associated with them, 1922–25, he wrote not a single story. It would take a student of American literature to recall a single work by Dorothy Parker, remembered today almost entirely for her outrageous witticisms at the table. George S. Kaufman went on to produce some of Broadway's greatest successes only after he pulled away from the group. Robert Benchley, regarded as a young genius, had to move out of the Algonquin in order to get any work done, by which time he already regretted that he had made himself into a public clown. Woollcott, once an enormously influential critic, is mainly recalled today, if at all, as the inspiration for the cantankerous and arrogant Sheridan Whiteside in *The Man Who Came to Dinner.*

As the most sophisticated New Yorkers of their era, noted for hilarious if brutal wit, they seem an unlikely source for mystery, crime, and suspense fiction, yet they produced a good deal of it. Most of it is humorous, as one might expect, and witty. Along with Lardner's often-anthologized "Haircut," which is one of the greatest stories of the twentieth century, the most famous crime story produced by a member of the Round Table (too long to include in this book) is *The Petrified Forest,* the Robert Sherwood play that starred Leslie Howard as Alan Squier, a failed, world-weary British intellectual, and made a star of the young Humphrey Bogart for his role as Duke Mantee, a desperate criminal. Both Howard and Bogart starred in the Warner Brothers film. Connelly's "Coroner's Verdict" won the O. Henry Prize in 1930.

The stories in this collection range from the silly and lightweight to the poignant and profound. There is little classic detection, not many realistic detectives, and less nail-biting suspense than in a more usual anthology. But the stories have charm, innocence, and a casual joyfulness that evoke another era, a time when music and laughter were part of the commonplace of daily life.

—OTTO PENZLER
New York, March 2007

Marc Connelly

Born December 13, 1885, in McKeesport, Pennsylvania, Marc Connelly was bitten by the drama bug early, composing his own plays at the age of five. He went on to become a journalist for the *Pittsburgh Sun* before moving to New York. He was one of the earliest members of the Algonquin Round Table and collaborated on several comedies with another enthusiastic member, George S. Kaufman: *Dulcy* (1921), *22 Little Old Millersville* (1921–22), *Merton of the Movies* (1922), and *Beggar on Horseback* (1925). *Merton of the Movies,* based on a 1922 novel by Harry Leon Wilson, was extremely successful, running for 392 performances on Broadway before going on the road.

His most important work was *Green Pastures* (1931), for which he won the Pulitzer Prize for drama. A retelling of the Old Testament, it was the first Broadway play to feature an all-black cast.

His autobiography, *Voices Offstage,* was published in 1968. He died December 21, 1980.

"Coroner's Inquest" was originally published in the February 8, 1930, issue of *Collier's.* It won the O. Henry Prize that year.

"I always knew children were anti-social. But the children of the West Side—they're savage."

—**Mark Connelly**

Coroner's Inquest

by **Mark Connelly**

"WHAT IS YOUR NAME?"

"Frank Wineguard."

"Where do you live?"

"A hundred and eighty-five West Fifty-fifth Street."

"What is your business?"

"I'm a stage manager for Hello, America."

"You were the employer of James Dawle?"

"In a way. We both worked for Mr. Bender, the producer, but I have charge backstage."

"Did you know Theodore Robel?"

"Yes, sir."

"Was he in your company, too?"

"No, sir. I met him when we started rehearsals. That was about three months ago, in June. We sent out a call for midgets and he and Jimmy showed up together, with a lot of others. Robel was too big for us. I didn't see him again until we broke into their room Tuesday."

"You discovered their bodies?"

"Yes, sir. Mrs. Pike, there, was with me."

"You found them both dead?"

"Yes, sir."

"How did you happen to be over in Jersey City?"

"Well, I'd called up his house at curtain time Monday night when I found Jimmy hadn't shown up for the performance. Mrs. Pike told me they were both out, and I asked her to have either Jimmy or Robel call me when they came in. Then Mrs. Pike called me Tuesday morning and said she tried to get into the room but she'd found the door was bolted. She said all the other roomers were out and she was alone and scared.

"I'd kind of suspected something might be wrong. So I said to wait and I'd come over. Then I took the tube over and got there about noon. Then we went up and I broke down the door."

"Did you see this knife there?"

"Yes, sir. It was on the floor, about a foot from Jimmy."

"You say you suspected something was wrong. What do you mean by that?"

"I mean I felt something might have happened to

Jimmy. Nothing like this, of course. But I knew he'd been feeling very depressed lately, and I know Robel wasn't helping to cheer him up any."

"You mean that they had had quarrels?"

"No, sir. They just both had the blues. Robel had had them for a long time. Robel was Jimmy's brother-in-law. He'd married Jimmy's sister—she was a midget, too—about five years ago, but she died a year or so later. Jimmy had been living with them and after the sister died he and Robel took a room in Mrs. Pike's house together."

"How did you learn this?"

"Jimmy and I were pretty friendly at the theater. He was a nice little fellow and seemed grateful that I'd given him his job. We'd only needed one midget for an Oriental scene in the second act and the agencies had sent about fifteen. Mr. Gehring, the director, told me to pick one of them as he was busy and I picked Jimmy because he was the littlest.

"After I got to know him he told me how glad he was I'd given him the job. He hadn't worked for nearly a year. He wasn't little enough to be a featured midget with circuses or in museums so he had to take whatever came along. Anyway, we got to be friendly and he used to tell me about his brother-in-law and all."

"He never suggested that there might be ill-feeling between him and his brother-in-law?"

"No, sir. I don't imagine he'd ever had any words at all with Robel. As a matter of fact from what I could gather I guess Jimmy had quite a lot of affection for him and he certainly did everything he could to help him. Robel was a lot worse off than Jimmy. Robel hadn't worked for a couple of years and Jimmy practically supported him. He used to tell me how Robel had been sunk ever since he got his late growth."

"His what?"

"His late growth. I heard it happens among midgets often, but Jimmy told me about it first. Usually a midget will stay as long as he lives at whatever height he reaches when he's fourteen or fifteen, but every now and then one of them starts growing again just before he's thirty, and he can grow a foot or even more in a couple years. Then he stops growing for good. But of course he don't look so much like a midget any more.

"That's what had happened to Robel about three years ago. Of course he had trouble getting jobs and it hit him pretty hard.

"From what Jimmy told me and from what Mrs. Pike says, I guess he used to talk about it all the time. Robel used to come over and see his agent in New York twice a week, but there was never anything for him. Then he'd go back to Jersey City. Most of the week he lived alone because after the show started Jimmy often stayed in

New York with a cousin or somebody that lived uptown.

"Lately Robel hadn't been coming over to New York at all. But every Saturday night Jimmy would go over to Jersey City and stay till Monday with him, trying to cheer him up. Every Sunday they'd take a walk and go to a movie. I guess as they walked along the street Robel realized most the difference in their heights. And I guess that's really why they're both dead now."

"How do you mean?"

"Well, as I told you, Jimmy would try to sympathize with Robel and cheer him up. He and Robel both realized that Jimmy was working and supporting them and that Jimmy would probably keep right on working, according to the ordinary breaks of the game, while Robel would always be too big. It simply preyed on Robel's mind.

"And then three weeks ago Monday Jimmy thought he saw the ax fall.

"I was standing outside the stage door—it was about seven-thirty—and Jimmy came down the alley. He looked down in the mouth, which I thought was strange seeing that he usually used to come in swinging his little cane and looking pretty cheerful. I said, 'How are you feeling, Jimmy?' and he said, 'I don't feel so good, Mr. Wineguard.' So I said, 'Why, what's the matter, Jimmy?' I could see there really was something the matter with him by this time.

" 'I'm getting scared,' he said, and I says, 'Why?'

" 'I'm starting to grow again,' he says. He said it the way you'd say you just found out you had some disease that was going to kill you in a week. He looked like he was shivering.

" 'Why, you're crazy, Jimmy,' I says. 'You ain't growing.'

" 'Yes, I am,' he says. 'I'm thirty-one and it's that late growth like my brother-in-law has. My father had it, but his people had money, so it didn't make much difference to him. It's different with me. I've got to keep working.'

"He went on like that for a while and then I tried to kid him out of it.

" 'You look all right to me,' I said. 'How tall have you been all along?'

" 'Thirty-seven inches,' he says. So I says, 'Come on into the prop-room and I'll measure you.'

"He backed away from me. 'No,' he says, 'I don't want to know how much it is.' Then he went up to the dressing-room before I could argue with him.

"All week he looked awful sunk. When he showed up the next Monday evening he looked almost white.

"I grabbed him as he was starting upstairs to make up.

" 'Come on out of it,' I says. I thought he'd make a break and try to get away from me, but he didn't. He just sort of smiled as if I didn't understand. Finally he says, 'It ain't any use, Mr. Wineguard.'

" 'Listen,' I says, 'you've been over with that brother-in-law of yours, haven't you?' He said yes, he had. 'Well,' I says, 'that's what's bothering you. From what you tell me about him, he's talked about his own tough luck so much that he's given you the willies, too. Stay away from him the end of this week.'

"He stood there for a second without saying anything. Then he says, 'That wouldn't do any good. He's all alone over there and he needs company. Anyway, it's all up with me, I guess. I've grown nearly two inches already.'

"I looked at him. He was pretty pathetic, but outside of that there wasn't any change in him as far as I could see.

"I says, 'Have you been measured?' He said he hadn't. Then I said, 'Then how do you know? Your clothes fit all right, except your pants and as a matter of fact, they seem a little longer.'

" 'I fixed my suspenders and let them down a lot farther,' he says. 'Besides, they were always a little big for me.'

" 'Let's make sure,' I says. 'I'll get a yard-stick and we'll make absolutely sure.'

"But I guess he was too scared to face things. He wouldn't do it.

"He managed to dodge me all week. Then, last Saturday night, I ran into him as I was leaving the theater. I asked him if he felt any better.

" 'I feel all right,' he says. He really looked scared to death.

"That's the last time I saw him before I went over to Jersey City after Mrs. Pike phoned me Tuesday."

"Patrolman Gorlitz has testified that the bodies were in opposite ends of the room when he arrived. They were in that position when you forced open the door?"

"Yes, sir."

"The medical examiner has testified that they were both dead of knife wounds, apparently from the same knife. Would you assume the knife had fallen from Dawle's hand as he fell?"

"Yes, sir."

"Has it been your purpose to suggest that both men were driven to despondency by a fear of lack of employment for Dawle, and that they might have committed suicide?"

"No, sir. I don't think anything of the kind."

"What do you mean?"

"Well, when Mrs. Pike and I went in the room and I got a look at the knife, I said to Mrs. Pike that that was a funny kind of a knife for them to have in the room. You can see it's a kind of a butcher knife. Then Mrs. Pike told me it was one that she'd missed from her kitchen a few weeks before. She'd never thought either Robel or Jimmy had taken it. It struck me as funny Robel or Jimmy had stolen it, too. Then I put two and two together and found out what really happened. Have you got the little broken cane that was lying on the bed?"

"Is this it?"

"Yes, sir. Well, I'd never been convinced by Jimmy that he was really growing. So when Mrs. Pike told me about the knife I started figuring. I figured that about five minutes before that knife came into play Jimmy must have found it, probably by accident."

"Why by accident?"

"Because Robel had gone a little crazy, I guess. He'd stolen it and kept it hidden from Jimmy. And when Jimmy found it he wondered what Robel been doing with it. Then Robel wouldn't tell him and Jimmy found out for himself. Or maybe Robel did tell him. Anyway, Jimmy looked at the came. It was the one he always carried. He saw where, when Jimmy wasn't looking, Robel had been *cutting little pieces off the end of it!*"

Robert Benchley

After attending Harvard, where he was editor of the *Harvard Lampoon,* Robert Benchley (1889–1945) moved to New York and took a job at *Vanity Fair,* sharing an office with Dorothy Parker. He then covered the theater for *Life* magazine, was a regular contributor to *The New Yorker,* and wrote a column three times a week for the Hearst newspapers. Many of his pieces were collected in such popular volumes as *Pluck and Luck* (1925), *From Bed to Worse* (1934) and *My Ten Years in a Quandary, and How They Grew* (1936).

He began to split his time between New York and Hollywood in the 1930s, writing and starring in numerous short features about the minor obstacles he faced during his day, always with himself as the brunt of the joke. In *How to Sleep,* he is seen tossing and turning as distractions prevent him from doing just that; it won the Academy Award for Best Short Subject in 1935. He was married to his childhood sweetheart, Gertrude Darling, from 1914 until his death of a cerebral hemorrhage in 1945. His son, Nathaniel Benchley, also became a successful writer, as did his grandson, Peter Benchley, the author of such megahits as *Jaws* and *The Island.*

"The Mystery of the Poisoned Kipper" was first collected in *No Poems, or Around the World Backwards and Sideways* in 1932.

"It took me fifteen years to discover that I had no talent for writing, but I couldn't give it up because by that time I was too famous."

—**Robert Benchley**

The Mystery of the Poisoned Kipper

by **Robert Benchley**

WHO SENT THE POISONED KIPPER to Major General Hannafield of the Royal Welch Lavaliers? That is the problem which is distorting Scotland Yard at the present moment, for the solution lies evidently in the breast of Major General Hannafield himself. And Major General Hannafield is dead. (At any rate, he doesn't answer his telephone.)

Following are the details, such as they are. You may take them or leave them. If you leave them, please leave them in the coat room downstairs and say that Martin will call for them.

One Saturday night about three weeks ago after a dinner given by the Royal Welch Lavaliers for the Royal Platinum Watch, Major General Hannafield returned home just in time for a late breakfast which he really didn't want. In fact, when his wife said, rather icily, "I suppose you've had your breakfast," the Maj Gen replied: "I'll thank you not to mention breakfast, *or* lunch, *or* dinner until such time as I give you the signal." Mrs. Hannafield thereupon packed her bags and left for her mother's in New Zealand.

Along about eleven-thirty in the morning, however, the Maj Gen extricated himself from the hatrack where he had gone to sleep, and decided that something rather drastic had to be done about his mouth. He thought of getting a new mouth; but as it was Sunday all the mouth shops were closed, and he had no chance of sending into London for anything. He thought of water, great tidal waves of water, but even that didn't seem to be exactly adequate. So naturally his mind turned next to kippered herring. "Send a thief to catch a thief," is an old saying but a good one, and applies especially to Sunday morning mouths.

So he rang for his man, and nobody answered.

The Maj Gen then went to the windows and called out to the gardener, who was wrestling with a dahlia, and suggested that he let those dahlias alone and see about getting a kipper, and what's more a very salty kipper, immediately. This the gardener did.

On receiving the kipper, the Maj Gen, according to

witnesses, devoured it with avidity, paper and all, and then hung himself back on the hatrack. This was the last that was seen of Major General Hannafield alive, although perhaps "alive" is too strong a word. Perhaps "breathing" would be better.

Mrs. Hannafield, being on her way to New Zealand, has been absolved of any connection with the crime (if causing the Maj Gen's death can be called a crime, as he was quite an offensive old gentleman). The gardener, from his cell in the Old Bailey, claims that he bought the kipper from a fish stall in the High Street, and the fish vender in the High Street claims that he bought the kipper from the gardener.

According to the officials of Scotland Yard, there are two possible solutions to the crime, neither of them probable: revenge, or inadvertent poisoning of the kipper in preparation. Both have been discarded, along with the remainder of the kipper.

Revenge as a motive is not plausible, as the only people who could possibly seek revenge on the Maj Gen were killed by him a long time ago. The Maj Gen was notoriously hot tempered, and, when opposed, was accustomed to settling his neck very low in his collar and rushing all the blood available to his temples. In such states as this he usually said: "Gad, sir!" and lashed out with an old Indian weapon which he always carried, killing his offender. He was always acquitted, on account of his war record.

It is quite possible that some relatives of one of the Maj Gen's victims might have tracked him from the Punjab or the Kit-Kat Club to his "diggings" on Diggings Street, but he usually was pretty careful to kill only people who were orphans or unmarried.

There was some thought at first that the Maj Gen might have at one time stolen the eye of an idol in India and brought it back to England, and that some zealot had followed him across the world and wreaked revenge on him. A study of the records, however, shows that the Maj Gen once tried to steal an emerald eye out of an Indian idol, but that the idol succeeded in getting the Maj Gen's eye instead, and that the Maj Gen came back to England wearing a glass eye—which accounted for his rather baffling mannerism of looking over a person's shoulder while that person was talking to him.

Now as for the inadvertent poisoning of a kipper in the process of being cured. Herring are caught off the coast of Normandy (they are also caught practically everywhere, but Normandy makes a better story), brought to shore by Norman fishermen dressed as Norman fishermen, and carried almost immediately to the Kipperers.

The herring kipperers are all under state control and

are examined by government agents both before and after kippering. They are subjected to the most rigid mental tests, and have to give satisfactory answers to such questions as "Do you believe in poisoning herring?" and "Which of the following statements is true? (a) William the Norman was really a Swede; (b) herring, placed in the handkerchief drawer, give the handkerchief that *je ne sais quoi*; (c) honesty is the best policy."

If the kipperers are able to answer these questions and can, in addition, chin themselves twelve times, they are allowed to proceed with their work. Otherwise they are sent to the French Chamber of Deputies, or Devil's Island, for ten years. So you can see that there is not much chance for a herring kipperer to go wrong, and practically no chance for Major General Hannafield to have been poisoned by mistake.

This leaves really nothing for Scotland Yard to work on, except an empty stomach. The motive of revenge being out, and accidental poisoning being out, the only possible solution remaining is that Major General Hannafield committed suicide by eating it. This theory they are working on, and at the coroner's inquest (which ought to come along any day now) the whole matter will be threshed out.

An examination of the Maj Gen's vital organs has disclosed nothing except a possible solution of the whereabout of the collier Cyclops, which was lost during the Great War.

Here the matter stands, or rather there. (It was here a minute ago.) Mrs. Hannafield may have some suggestions to offer, if she ever will land in New Zealand, but according to radio dispatches she is having an awfully good time on the boat and keeps going back and forth without ever getting off when they put into port. She and the ship's doctor have struck up an acquaintance, and you know what that means.

S. J. Perelman

Born on February 1, 1900, Sidney Joseph Perelman is mainly famous for the huge number of brief comic pieces he wrote for *The New Yorker* for many years, as well as hilarious screenplays, most notably *Horse Feathers* and *Animal Crackers* for the Marx Brothers. He won an Academy Award for his screenplay for *Around the World in Eighty Days.* His most successful Broadway play was *One Touch of Venus,* for which he cowrote the book with Ogden Nash; Kurt Weill wrote the music and Nash the lyrics. It ran for more than 500 performances and was made into a popular motion picture starring Ava Gardner and Robert Walker.

As is true of the sketches in this book, his short prose works cannot accurately be called short stories. They are almost unique to Perelman: filled with ridicule (often with himself as the target), irony, and satire, using news stories, literary and theatrical works and, mainly, his own experiences as the subjects for pieces. A frequent visitor at the Round Table, he cowrote a play, *The Dark Tower,* with Alexander Woollcott. He died in 1979.

In the *Oxford Book of Humorous Prose,* an important study of humor, the British writer Frank Muir named Perelman the best American comic author of all time—an assessment that undoubtedly would be challenged by aficionados of Mark Twain.

After buying rural property in Bucks County, Pennysylvania: "A farm is an irregular patch of nettles bound by short-term notes, containing a fool and his wife who didn't know enough to stay in the city."

—**S. J. Perelman**

Farewell, My Lovely Appetizer

by **S. J. Perelman**

Add Smorgasbits to your ought-to-know department, the newest of the three Betty Lee products. What in the world! Just small mouth-size pieces of herring and of pinkish tones. We crossed our heart and promised not to tell the secret of their tinting.

—Clementine Paddleford's food column in the Herald Tribune.

The "Hush-Hush" Blouse. We're very hush-hush about his name, but the celebrated shirtmaker who did it for us is famous on two continents for blouses with details like those deep yoke folds, the wonderful shoulder pads, the shirtband bow!

—Russeks adv. in the Times.

I CAME DOWN THE SIXTH-FLOOR CORRIDOR of the Arbogast Building, past the World Wide Noodle Corporation, Zwinger & Rumsey, Accountants, and the Ace Secretarial Service, Mimeographing Our Specialty. The legend on the ground-glass panel next door said, "Atlas Detective Agency, Noonan & Driscoll," but Snapper Driscoll had retired two years before with a .38 slug between the shoulders, donated by a snowbird in Tacoma, and I owned what good will the firm had. I let myself into the crummy anteroom we kept to impress clients, growled good morning at Birdie Claflin.

"Well, you certainly look like something the cat dragged in," she said. She had a quick tongue. She also had eyes like dusty lapis lazuli, taffy hair, and a figure that did things to me. I kicked open the bottom drawer of her desk, let two inches of rye trickle down my craw, kissed Birdie square on her lush, red mouth, and set fire to a cigarette.

"I could go for you, sugar," I said slowly. Her face was veiled, watchful. I stared at her ears, liking the way they were joined to her head. There was something complete about them; you knew they were there for keeps. When you're a private eye, you want things to stay put.

"Any customers?"

"A woman by the name of Sigrid Bjornsterne said she'd be back. A looker."

"Swede?"

"She'd like you to think so."

I nodded toward the inner office to indicate that I was going in there, and went in there. I lay down on the davenport, took off my shoes, and bought myself a shot from the bottle I kept underneath. Four minutes later, an ash blonde with eyes the color of unset opals, in a Nettie Rosenstein basic black dress and a baum-marten stole, burst in. Her bosom was heaving and it looked even better that way. With a gasp she circled the desk, hunting for some place to hide, and then, spotting the wardrobe where I keep a change of bourbon, ran into it. I got up and wandered out into the anteroom. Birdie was deep in a crossword puzzle.

"See anyone come in here?"

"Nope." There was a thoughtful line between her brows. "Say, what's a five-letter word meaning 'trouble'?"

"Swede," I told her, and went back inside. I waited the length of time it would take a small, not very bright boy to recite "Ozymandias," and, inching carefully along the wall, took a quick gander out the window. A thin galoot with stooping shoulders was being very busy reading a paper outside the Gristede store two blocks away. He hadn't been there an hour ago, but then, of course, neither had I. He wore a size-seven dove-colored hat from Browning King, a tan Wilson Brothers shirt with pale-blue stripes, a J. Press foulard with a mixed-red-and-white figure, dark blue Interwoven socks, and an unshined pair of ox-blood London Character shoes. I let a cigarette burn down between my fingers until it made a small red mark, and then I opened the wardrobe.

"Hi," the blonde said lazily. "You Mike Noonan?" I made a noise that could have been "Yes," and waited. She yawned. I thought things over, decided to play it safe. I yawned. She yawned back, then, settling into a corner of the wardrobe, went to sleep. I let another cigarette burn down until it made a second red mark beside the first one, and then I woke her up. She sank into a chair, crossing a pair of gams that tightened my throat as I peered under the desk at them.

"Mr. Noonan," she said, "you—you've got to help me."

"My few friends call me Mike," I said pleasantly.

"Mike." She rolled the syllable on her tongue. "I don't believe I've ever heard that name before. Irish?"

"Enough to know the difference between a gossoon and a bassoon."

"What *is* the difference?" she asked. I dummied up; I figured I wasn't giving anything away for free. Her eyes narrowed. I shifted my two hundred pounds slightly, lazily set fire to a finger, and watched it burn down. I could see she was admiring the interplay of muscles in my shoulders. There wasn't any extra fat on Mike Noonan, but I wasn't telling *her* that. I was playing it safe until I knew where we stood.

When she spoke again, it came with a rush. "Mr. Noonan, he thinks I'm trying to poison him. But I swear the herring was pink—I took it out of the jar myself. If I could only find out how they tinted it. I offered them money, but they wouldn't tell."

"Suppose you take it from the beginning," I suggested.

She drew a deep breath. "You've heard of the golden spintria of Hadrian?" I shook my head. "It's a tremendously valuable coin believed to have been given by the Emperor Hadrian to one of his proconsuls, Caius Vitellius. It disappeared about 150 A.D., and eventually passed into the possession of Hucbald the Fat. After the sack of Adrianople by the Turks, it was loaned by a man named Shapiro to the court physician, or hakim, of Abdul Mahmoud. Then it dropped out of sight for nearly five hundred years, until last August, when a dealer in second-hand books named Lloyd Thursday sold it to my husband."

"And now it's gone again," I finished.

"No," she said. "At least, it was lying on the dresser when I left, an hour ago." I leaned back, pretending to fumble a carbon out of the desk, and studied her legs again. This was going to be a lot more intricate than I had thought. Her voice got huskier. "Last night I brought home a jar of Smorgasbits for Walter's dinner. You know them?"

"Small mouth-size pieces of herring and of pinkish tones, aren't they?"

Her eyes darkened, lightened, got darker again. "How did you know?"

"I haven't been a private op nine years for nothing, sister. Go on."

"I—I knew right away something was wrong when Walter screamed and upset his plate. I tried to tell him the herring was supposed to be pink, but he carried on like a madman. He's been suspicious of me since—well, ever since I made him take out that life insurance."

"What was the face amount of the policy?"

"A hundred thousand. But it carried a triple-indemnity clause in case he died by sea food. Mr. Noonan—Mike"—her tone caressed me—"I've got to win back his confidence. You could find out how they tinted that herring."

"What's in it for me?"

"Anything you want." The words were a whisper. I leaned over, poked open her handbag, counted off five grand.

"This'll hold me for a while," I said. "If I need any more, I'll beat my spoon on the high chair." She got up. "Oh, while I think of it, how does this golden spintria of yours tie in with the herring?"

"It doesn't," she said calmly. "I just threw it in for glamour." She trailed past me in a cloud of scent that retailed at ninety rugs the ounce. I caught her wrist, pulled her up to me.

"I go for girls named Sigrid with opal eyes," I said.

"Where'd you learn my name?"

"I haven't been a private snoop twelve years for nothing, sister."

"It was nine last time."

"It seemed like twelve till *you* came along." I held the clinch until a faint wisp of smoke curled out of her ears, pushed her through the door. Then I slipped a pint of rye into my stomach and a heater into my kick and went looking for a bookdealer named Lloyd Thursday. I knew he had no connection with the herring caper, but in my business you don't overlook anything.

The thin galoot outside Gristede's had taken a powder when I got there; that meant we were no longer playing girls' rules. I hired a hack to Wanamaker's, cut over to Third, walked up toward Fourteenth. At Twelfth a mink-faced jasper made up as a street cleaner tailed me for a block, drifted into a dairy restaurant. At Thirteenth somebody dropped a sour tomato out of a third-story window, missing me by inches. I doubled back to Wanamaker's, hopped a bus up Fifth to Madison Square, and switched to a cab down Fourth, where the second-hand bookshops elbow each other like dirty urchins.

A flabby hombre in a Joe Carbondale rope-knit sweater, whose jowl could have used a shave, quit giggling over the Heptameron long enough to tell me he was Lloyd Thursday. His shoe-button eyes became opaque when I asked to see any first editions or incunabula relative to the *Clupea harengus,* or common herring.

"You got the wrong pitch, copper," he snarled, "That stuff is hotter than Pee Wee Russell's clarinet."

"Maybe a sawbuck'll smarten you up," I said. I folded one to the size of a postage stamp, scratched my chin with it. "There's five yards around for anyone who knows why those Smorgasbits of Sigrid Bjornsterne's happened to be pink." His eyes got crafty.

"I might talk for a grand."

"Start dealing." He motioned toward the back. I took a step forward. A second later a Roman candle exploded inside my head and I went away from there. When I came to, I was on the floor with a lump on my sconce the size of a lapwing's egg and big Terry Tremaine of Homicide was bending over me.

"Someone sapped me," I said thickly. "His name was—"

"Webster," grunted Terry. He held up a dog-eared copy of Merriam's Unabridged. "You tripped on a loose board and this fell off a shelf on your think tank."

"Yeah?" I said skeptically. "Then where's Thursday?" He pointed to the fat man lying across a pile of erotica. "He passed out cold when he saw you cave." I covered up, let Terry figure it any way he wanted. I wasn't telling him what cards I held. I was playing it safe until I knew all the angles.

In a seedy pharmacy off Astor Place, a stale Armenian, whose name might have been Vulgarian but wasn't, dressed my head and started asking questions. I put my knee in his groin and he lost interest. Jerking my head toward the coffee urn, I spent a nickel and the next forty minutes doing some heavy thinking. Then I holed up in a phone booth and dialled a clerk I knew called Little Farvel, in a delicatessen store on Amsterdam Avenue. It took a while to get the dope I wanted because the connection was bad and Little Farvel had been dead two years, but we Noonans don't let go easily.

By the time I worked back to the Arbogast Building, via the Weehawken ferry and the George Washington Bridge to cover my tracks, all the pieces were in place. Or so I thought up to the point she came out of the wardrobe holding me between the sights of her ice-blue automatic.

"Reach for the stratosphere, gumshoe." Sigrid Bjornsterne's voice was colder than Horace Greeley and Little Farvel put together, but her clothes were plenty calorific. She wore a forest-green suit of Hockanum woollens, a Knox Wayfarer, and baby crocodile pumps. It was her blouse, though, that made tiny red hairs stand up on my knuckles. Its deep yoke folds, shoulder pads, and shirtband bow could only have been designed by some master craftsman, some Cézanne of the shears.

"Well, Nosy Parker," she sneered, "so you found out how they tinted the herring."

"Sure—grenadine," I said easily. "You knew it all along. And you planned to add a few grains of oxylbutanecheriphosphate, which turns the same shade of pink in solution, to your husband's portion, knowing it wouldn't show in the post-mortem. Then you'd collect the three hundred g's and join Harry Pestalozzi in Nogales till the heat died down. But you didn't count on me."

"You?" Mockery nicked her full-throated laugh. "What are you going to do about it?"

"This." I snaked the rug out from under her and she went down in a swirl of silken ankles. The bullet whined by me into the ceiling as I vaulted over the desk, pinioned her against the wardrobe.

"Mike." Suddenly all the hatred had drained away and her body yielded to mine. "Don't turn me in. You cared for me—once."

"It's no good, Sigrid. You'd only double-time me again."

"Try me."

"O.K. The shirtmaker who designed your blouse—what's his name?" A shudder of fear went over her; she averted her head. "He's famous on two continents. Come on Sigrid, they're your dice."

"I won't tell you. I can't, it's a secret between this—this department store and me."

"They wouldn't be loyal to *you.* They'd sell you out fast enough."

"Oh, Mike, you mustn't. You don't know what you're asking."

"For the last time."

"Oh, sweetheart, don't you see?" Her eyes were tragic pools, a cenotaph to lost illusions. "I've got so little. Don't take that away from me. I—I'd never be able to hold up my head in Russeks again."

"Well, if that's the way you want to play it . . ." There

was silence in the room, broken only by Sigrid's choked sob. Then, with a strangely empty feeling, I uncradled the phone and dialled Spring 7-3100.

For an hour after they took her away, I sat alone in the taupe-colored dusk, watching lights come on and a woman in the hotel opposite adjusting a garter. Then I treated my tonsils to five fingers of firewater, jammed on my hat, and made for the anteroom. Birdie was still scowling over her crossword puzzle. She looked up crookedly at me.

"Need me any more tonight?"

"No." I dropped a grand or two in her lap. "Here, buy yourself some Stardust."

"Thanks, I've got my quota." For the first time I caught a shadow of pain behind her eyes. "Mike, would—would you tell me something?"

"As long as it isn't clean," I flipped to conceal my bitterness.

"What's an eight-letter word meaning 'sentimental'?"

"Flatfoot, darling," I said, and went out into the rain.

Ring Lardner

Although not "officially" a member of the Algonquin Round Table (there were, of course, no official members), Ring Lardner, born in Niles, Michigan, in 1885, was one of the most important writers associated with the group. By the time the Round Table was established, Lardner, unlike most of its members, had already become a successful journalist and fiction writer, beginning as a sports columnist for several newspapers and finally the *Chicago Tribune.* His short stories soon appeared in the prestigious pages of *The Saturday Evening Post* and *Esquire.*

After moving to Great Neck, New York, in 1920, Lardner and his wife became close friends with F. Scott Fitzgerald and his wife, Zelda, helping to edit *The Great Gatsby* while Scott helped Lardner put together his first successful book, *How to Write Short Stories.* Although of radically different personalities, the taciturn Lardners and the highly social Fitzgeralds, undoubtedly bound by their love of alcohol, remained close friends for many years. Both writers died young, Lardner in 1933 at the age of 48.

As was true of many Round Tablers, Lardner collaborated with George S. Kaufman on a play, *June Moon.* Such short stories as "Haircut," "Alibi Ike," and the collection *You Know Me Al* feature simple, uneducated characters, utterly lacking in self-awareness, who nonetheless were much-loved by readers and often were compared with Damon Runyon's work.

"He gave her a look that you could have poured on a waffle."

—**Ring Lardner**

Haircut

by **Ring Lardner**

I GOT *ANOTHER* BARBER that comes over from Carterville and helps me out Saturdays, but the rest of the time I can get along all right alone. You can see for yourself that this ain't no New York City and besides that, the most of the boys works all day and don't have no leisure to drop in here and get themselves prettied up.

You're a newcomer, ain't you? I thought I hadn't seen you round before. I hope you like it good enough to stay. As I say, we ain't no New York City or Chicago, but we have pretty good times. Not as good, though, since Jim Kendall got killed. When he was alive, him and Hod Meyers used to keep this town in an uproar. I bet they was more laughin' done here than any town its size in America.

Jim was comical, and Hod was pretty near a match for him. Since Jim's gone, Hod tries to hold his end up just the same as ever, but it's tough goin' when you ain't got nobody to kind of work with.

They used to be plenty fun in here Saturdays. This place is jam-packed Saturdays, from four o'clock on. Jim and Hod would show up right after their supper, round six o'clock. Jim would set himself down in that big chair, nearest the blue spittoon. Whoever had been settin' in that chair, why they'd get up when Jim come in and give it to him.

You'd of thought it was a reserved seat like they have sometimes in a theayter. Hod would generally always stand or walk up and down, or some Saturdays, of course, he'd be settin' in his chair part of the time, gettin' a haircut.

Well, Jim would set there a w'ile without openin' his mouth only to spit, and then finally he'd say to me, "Whitey"—my right name, that is, my right first name, is Dick, but everybody round here calls me Whitey—Jim would say, "Whitey, your nose looks like a rosebud tonight. You must of been drinkin' some of your aw de cologne."'

So I'd say. "No, Jim, but you look like you'd been drinkin' somethin' of that kind or somethin' worse."

Jim would have to laugh at that, but then he'd speak

up and say, "No, I ain't had nothin' to drink, but that ain't sayin' I wouldn't like somethin'. I wouldn't even mind if it was wood alcohol."

Then Hod Meyers would say, "Neither would your wife." That would set everybody to laughin' because Jim and his wife wasn't on very good terms. She'd of divorced him only they wasn't no chance to get alimony and she didn't have no way to take care of herself and the kids. She couldn't never understand Jim. He *was* kind of rough, but a good fella at heart.

Him and Hod had all kinds of sport with Milt Sheppard. I don't suppose you've seen Milt. Well, he's got an Adam's apple that looks more like a mushmelon. So I'd shavin' Milt and when I'd start to shave down here on his neck, Hod would holler, "Hey, Whitey, wait a minute! Before you cut into it, let's make up a pool and see who can guess closest to the number of seeds."

And Jim would say, "If Milt hadn't of been so hoggish, he'd of ordered a half a cantaloupe instead of a whole one and it might not of stuck in his throat."

All the boys would roar at this and Milt himself would force a smile, though the joke was on him. Jim certainly was a card!

There's his shavin' mug, settin' on the shelf, right next to Charley Vail's. "Charles M. Vail." That's the druggist. He comes in regular for his shave, three times a week. And Jim's is the cup next to Charley's. "James H. Kendall." Jim won't need no shavin' mug no more, but I'll leave it there just the same for old time's sake. Jim certainly was a character!

Years ago, Jim used to travel for a canned goods concern over in Carterville. They sold canned goods. Jim had the whole northern half of the state and was on the road five days out of every week. He'd drop in here Saturdays and tell his experiences for that week. It was rich.

I guess he paid more attention to playin' jokes than makin' sales. Finally the concern let him out and he come right home here and told everybody he'd been fired instead of sayin' he'd resigned like most fellas would of.

It was a Saturday and the shop was full and Jim got up out of that chair and says, "Gentlemen, I got an important announcement to make. I been fired from my job."

Well, they asked him if he was in earnest and he said he was and nobody could think of nothin' to say till Jim finally broke the ice himself. He says, "I been sellin' canned goods and now I'm canned goods myself."

You see, the concern he'd been workin' for was a factory that made canned goods. Over in Carterville. And now Jim said he was canned himself. He was certainly a card!

Jim had a great trick that he used to play w'ile he was travelin'. For instance, he'd be ridin' on a train and they'd come to some little town like, well, like, we'll say, like Benton. Jim would look out the train window and read the signs on the stores.

For instance, they'd be a sign, "Henry Smith, Dry Goods." Well, Jim would write down the name and the name of the town and when he got to wherever he was goin' he'd mail back a postal card to Henry Smith at Benton and not sign no name to it, but he'd write on the card, well, somethin' like "Ask your wife about that book agent that spent the afternoon last week," or "Ask your Missus who kept her from gettin' lonesome the last time you was in Carterville." And he'd sign the card, "A Friend." Of course, he never knew what really come of none of those jokes, but he could picture what *probably* happened and that was enough. Jim didn't work very steady after he lost his position with the Carterville people. What he did earn, doin' odd jobs round town, why he spent pretty near all of it on gin and his family might of starved if the stores hadn't of carried them along. Jim's wife tried her hand at dress-makin', but they ain't nobody goin' to get rich makin' dresses in this town.

As I say, she'd of divorced Jim, only she seen that she couldn't support herself and the kids and she was always hopin' that some day Jim would cut out his habits and give her more than two or three dollars a week.

They was a time when she would go to whoever he was workin' for and ask them to give her his wages, but after she done this once or twice, he beat her to it by borrowin' most of his pay in advance. He told it all round town, how he had outfoxed his Missus. He certainly was a caution!

But he wasn't satisfied with just outwittin' her. He was sore the way she had acted, tryin' to grab off his pay. And he made up his mind he'd get even. Well, he waited till Evans's Circus was advertised to come to town. Then he told his wife and two kiddies that he was goin' to take them to the circus. The day of the circus, he told them he would get the tickets and meet them outside the entrance to the tent. Well, he didn't have no intentions of bein' there or buyin' tickets or nothin'. He got full of gin and laid round Wright's poolroom all day. His wife and kids waited and waited and of course he didn't show up. His wife didn't have a dime with her, or nowhere else, I guess. So she finally had to tell the kids it was all off and they cried like they wasn't never goin' to stop.

Well, it seems, w'ile they was cryin', Doc Stair came along and he asked what was the matter, but Mrs. Kendall was stubborn and wouldn't tell him, but the kids told him and he insisted on takin' them and their mother in to the show. Jim found this out afterwards and it was one reason why he had it in for Doc Stair.

Doc Stair come here about a year and a half ago. He's a mighty handsome young fella and his clothes always look like he has them made to order. He goes to Detroit two or three times a year and w'ile he's there he must have a tailor take his measure and then make him a suit to order. They cost pretty near twice as much, but they fit a whole lot better than if you just bought them in a store.

For a w'ile everybody was wonderin' why a young doctor like Doc Stair should come to a town like this where we already got old Doc Gamble and Doc Foote that's both been here for years and all the practice in town was always divided between the two of them.

Then they was a story got round that Doc Stair's gal had throwed him over, a gal up in the Northern Peninsula somewheres, and the reason he come here was to hide himself away and forget it. He said himself that he thought they wasn't nothin' like general practice in a place like ours to fit a man to be a good all round doctor. And that's why he'd came.

Anyways, it wasn't long before he was makin' enough to live on, though they tell me that he never dunned nobody for what they owed him, and the folks here certainly has got the owin' habit, even in my business. If I had all that was comin' to me for just shaves alone, I could go to Carterville and put up at the Mercer for a week and see a different picture every night. For instance, they's old George Purdy—but I guess I shouldn't ought to be gossipin'.

Well, last year, our coroner died, died of the flu. Ken Beatty, that was his name. He was the coroner. So they had to choose another man to be coroner in his place and they picked Doc Stair. He laughed at first and said he didn't want it, but they made him take it. It ain't no job that anybody would fight for and what a man makes out of it in a year would just about buy seeds for their garden. Doc's the kind, though, that can't say no to nothin' if you keep at him long enough.

But I was goin' to tell you about a poor boy we got here in town—Paul Dickson. He fell out of a tree when he was about ten years old. Lit on his head and it done somethin' to him and he ain't never been right. No harm in him, but just silly. Jim Kendall used to call him cuckoo; that's a name Jim had for anybody that was off their head, only he called people's head their bean. That was another of his gags, callin' head bean and callin' crazy people cuckoo. Only poor Paul ain't crazy, but just silly.

You can imagine that Jim used to have all kinds of fun with Paul. He'd send him to the White Front Garage for a left-handed monkey wrench. Of course they ain't no such a thing as a left-handed monkey wrench.

And once we had a kind of a fair here and they was a baseball game between the fats and the leans and before the game started Jim called Paul over and sent him way down to Schrader's hardware store to get a key for the pitcher's box.

They wasn't nothin' in the way of gags that Jim couldn't think up, when he put his mind to it.

Poor Paul was always kind of suspicious of people, maybe on account of how Jim had kept foolin' him. Paul wouldn't have much to do with anybody only his own mother and Doc Stair and a girl here in town named Julie Gregg. That is, she ain't a girl no more, but pretty near thirty or over.

When Doc first came to town, Paul seemed to feel like here was a real friend and he hung around Doc's office most of the w'ile; the only time he wasn't there was when he'd go home to eat or sleep or when he seen Julie Gregg doin' her shoppin'.

When he looked out Doc's window and seen her, he'd run downstairs and join her and tag along with her to the different stores. The poor boy was crazy about Julie and she always treated him mighty nice and made him feel like he was welcome, though of course it wasn't nothin' but pity on her side.

Doc done all he could to improve Paul's mind and he told me once that he really thought the boy was gettin' better, that they was times when he was as bright and sensible as anybody else.

But I was goin' to tell you about Julie Gregg. Old Man Gregg was in the lumber business, but got to drinkin' and lost the most of his money and when he died, he didn't leave nothin' but the house and just enough insurance for the girl to skimp along on.

Her mother was a kind of a half invalid and didn't hardly ever leave the house. Julie wanted to sell the place and move somewheres else after the old man died, but the mother said she was born here and would die here. It was tough on Julie, as the young people round this town—well, she's too good for them.

She's been away to school and Chicago and New York and different places and they ain't no subject she can't talk on, where you take the rest of the young folks here and you mention anything to them outside of Gloria Swanson or Tommy Meighan and they think you're delirious. Did you see Gloria in *Wages of Virtue*? You missed somethin'!

Well, Doc Stair hadn't been here more than a week

when he come in one day to get shaved and I recognized who he was as he had been pointed out to me, so I told him about my old lady. She's been ailin' for a couple years and either Doc Gamble or Doc Foote, neither one, seemed to be helpin' her. So he said he would come out and see her, but if she was able to get out herself, it would be better to bring her to his office where he could make a complete examination.

So I took her to his office and w'ile I was waiting' for her in the reception room, in come Julie Gregg. When somebody comes in Doc Stair's office, they's a bell that rings in his inside office so he can tell they's somebody to see him.

So he left my old lady inside and come out to the front office and that's the first time him and Julie met and I guess it was what they call love at first sight. But it wasn't fifty-fifty. This young fella was the slickest lookin' fella she'd ever seen in this town and she went wild over him. To him she was just a young lady that wanted to see the doctor.

She'd came on about the same business I had. Her mother had been doctorin' for years with Doc Gamble and Doc Foote and with no results. So she'd heard they was a new doc in town and decided to give him a try. He promised to call and see her mother that same day.

I said a minute ago that it was love at first sight on her part. I'm not only judgin' by how she acted afterwards but how she looked at him that first day in his office. I ain't no mind reader, but it was wrote all over her face that she was gone.

Now Jim Kendall, besides bein' a jokesmith and a pretty good drinker, well, Jim was quite a lady-killer. I guess he run pretty wild durin' the time he was on the road for them Carterville people, and besides that, he'd had a couple little affairs of the heart right here in town. As I say, his wife could of divorced him, only she couldn't. But Jim was like the majority of men, and women, too, I guess. He wanted what he couldn't get. He wanted Julie Gregg and worked his head off tryin' to land her. Only he'd of said bean instead of head.

Well, Jim's habits and his jokes didn't appeal to Julie and of course he was a married man, so he didn't have no more chance than, well, than a rabbit. That's an expression of Jim's himself. When somebody didn't have no chance to get elected or somethin', Jim would always say they didn't have no more chance than a rabbit. He didn't make no bones about how he felt. Right in here, more than once, in front of the whole crowd, he said he was stuck on Julie and anybody that could get her for him was welcome to his house and his wife and kids included. But she wouldn't have nothin' to do with him; wouldn't even speak to him on the street. He finally seen he wasn't gettin' nowheres with his usual line so he decided to try the rough stuff. He went right up to her house one evenin' and when she opened the door he forced his way in and grabbed her. But she broke loose and before he could stop her, she run in the next room and locked the door and phoned to Joe Barnes. Joe's the marshal. Jim could hear who she was phonin' to and he beat it before Joe got there.

Joe was an old friend of Julie's pa. Joe went to Jim the next day and told him what would happen if he ever done it again.

I don't know how the news of this little affair leaked out. Chances is that Joe Barnes told his wife and she told somebody else's wife and they told their husband. Anyways, it did leak out and Hod Meyers had the nerve to kid Jim about it, right here in this shop. Jim didn't deny nothin' and kind of laughed it off and said for us all to wait; that lots of people had tried to make a monkey out of him, but he always got even.

Meanw'ile everybody in town was wise to Julie's bein' wild mad over the Doc. I don't suppose she had any idea how her face changed when him and her was together; of course she couldn't of, or she'd kept away from him. And she didn't know that we was all noticin' how many times she made excuses to go up to his office or pass it on the other side of the street and look up in his window to see if he was there. I felt sorry for her and so did most other people.

Hod Meyers kept rubbin' it into Jim about how the Doc had cut him out. Jim didn't pay no attention to the kiddin' and you could see he was plannin' one of his jokes.

One trick Jim had was the knack of changin' his voice. He could make you think he was a girl talkin' and he could mimic any man's voice. To show you how good he was along this line, I'll tell you the joke he played on me once.

You know, in most towns of any size, when a man is dead and needs a shave, why the barber that shaves him soaks him five dollars for the job; that is, he don't soak *him,* but whoever ordered the shave. I just charge three dollars because personally I don't mind much shavin' a dead person. They lay a whole lot stiller than live customers. The only thing is that you don't feel like talkin' to them and you get kind of lonesome.

Well, about the coldest day we ever had here, two years ago last winter, the phone rung at the house w'ile I was home to dinner and I answered the phone and it was a woman's voice and she said she was Mrs. John Scott and her husband was dead and would I come out and shave him.

Old John had always been a good customer of mine. But they live seven miles out in the country, on the Streeter road. Still I didn't see how I could say no.

So I said I would be there, but would have to come in a jitney and it might cost three or four dollars besides the price of the shave. So she, or the voice, it said that was all right, so I got Frank Abbott to drive me out to the place and when I got there, who should open the door but old John himself! He wasn't no more dead than, well, than a rabbit.

It didn't take no private detective to figure out who had played me this little joke. Nobody could of thought it up but Jim Kendall. He certainly was a card!

I tell you this incident just to show you how he could disguise his voice and make you believe it was somebody else talkin'. I'd of swore it was Mrs. Scott had called me. Anyways, some woman.

Well, Jim waited till he had Doc Stair's voice down pat; then he went after revenge.

He called Julie up on a night when he knew Doc was over in Carterville. She never questioned but what it was Doc's voice. Jim said he must see her that night; he couldn't wait no longer to tell her somethin'. She was all excited and told him to come to the house. But he said he was expectin' an important long distance call and wouldn't she please forget her manners for once and come to his office. He said they couldn't nothin' hurt her and nobody would see her and he just *must* talk to her a little w'ile. Well, poor Julie fell for it.

Doc always keeps a night light in his office, so it looked to Julie like they was somebody there.

Meanw'ile Jim Kendall had went to Wright's poolroom, where they was a whole gang amusin' themselves. The most of them had drank plenty of gin, and they was a rough bunch even when sober. They was always strong for Jim's jokes and when he told them to come with him and see some fun they give up their card games and pool games and followed along.

Doc's office is on the second floor. Right outside his door they's a flight of stairs leadin' to the floor above. Jim and his gang hid in the dark behind these stairs.

Well, Julie come up to Doc's door and rung the bell and they was nothin' doin'. She rung it again and she rung it seven or eight times. Then she tried the door and found it locked. Then Jim made some kind of a noise and she heard it and waited a minute, and then she says, "Is that you, Ralph?" Ralph is Doc's first name.

They was no answer and it must of came to her all of a sudden that she'd been bunked. She pretty near fell downstairs and the whole gang after her. They chased her all the way home, hollerin', "Is that you, Ralph?"

and "Oh, Ralphie, dear, is that you?" Jim says he couldn't holler it himself, as he was laughin' too hard.

Poor Julie! She didn't show up here on Main Street for a long, long time afterward.

And of course Jim and his gang told everybody in town, everybody but Doc Stair. They was scared to tell him, and he might of never knowed only for Paul Dickson. The poor cuckoo, as Jim called him, he was here in the shop one night when Jim was still gloatin' yet over what he'd done to Julie. And Paul took in as much of it as he could understand and he run to Doc with the story.

It's a cinch Doc went up in the air and swore he'd make Jim suffer. But it was a kind of a delicate thing, because if it got out that he had beat Jim up, Julie was bound to hear of it and then she'd know that Doc knew and of course knowin' that he knew would make it worse for her than ever. He was goin' to do somethin', but it took a lot of figurin'.

Well, it was a couple of days later when Jim was here in the shop again, and so was the cuckoo. Jim was goin' duck-shootin' the next day and had come in lookin' for Hod Meyers to go with him. I happened to know that Hod had went over to Carterville and wouldn't be home till the end of the week. So Jim said he hated to go alone and he guessed he would call it off. Then poor Paul spoke up and said if Jim would take him he would go along. Jim thought a w'ile and then he said, well, he guessed a half-wit was better than nothin'.

I suppose he was plottin' to get Paul out in the boat and play some joke on him, like pushin' him in the water. Anyways, he said Paul could go. He asked him had he ever shot a duck and Paul said no, he'd never even had a gun in his hands. So Jim said he could set in the boat and watch him and if he behaved himself, he might lend him his gun for a couple of shots. They made a date to meet in the mornin' and that's the last I seen of Jim alive.

Next mornin', I hadn't been open more than ten minutes when Doc Stair come in. He looked kind of nervous. He asked me had I seen Paul Dickson. I said no, but I knew where he was, out duck-shootin' with Jim Kendall. So Doc says that's what he had heard, and he couldn't understand it because Paul had told him he wouldn't never have no more to do with Jim as long as he lived.

He said Paul had told him about the joke Jim had played on Julie. He said Paul had asked him what he thought of the joke and the Doc had told him that anybody that would do a thing like that ought not to be let live.

I said it had been a kind of a raw thing, but Jim just

couldn't resist no kind of a joke, no matter how raw. I said I thought he was all right at heart, but just bubblin' over with mischief. Doc turned and walked out.

At noon he got a phone call from old John Scott. The lake where Jim and Paul had went shootin' is on John's place. Paul had came runnin' up to the house a few minutes before and said they'd been an accident. Jim had shot a few ducks and then give the gun to Paul and told him to try his luck. Paul hadn't never handled a gun and he was nervous. He was shakin' so hard that he couldn't control the gun. He let fire and Jim sunk back in the boat, dead.

Doc Stair, bein' the coroner, jumped in Frank Abbott's flivver and rushed out to Scott's farm. Paul and old John was down on the shore of the lake. Paul had rowed the boat to shore, but they'd left the body in it, waitin' for Doc to come.

Doc examined the body and said they might as well fetch it back to town. They was no use leavin' it there or callin' a jury, as it was a plain case of accidental shootin'.

Personally I wouldn't never leave a person shoot a gun in the same boat I was in unless I was sure they knew somethin' about guns. Jim was a sucker to leave a new beginner have his gun, let alone a half-wit. It probably served Jim right, what he got. But still we miss him round here. He certainly was a card!

Comb it wet or dry?

ALEXANDER WOOLLCOTT

Though not much read today, "Aleck" Woollcott was a hugely influential critic in his day, both of the theater and literature, single-handedly making James Hilton's *Goodbye, Mr. Chips* and *Lost Horizon* best-sellers. Born January 19, 1887, in Phalanx, New Jersey, he became a prolific drama critic for *The New York Times* and then wrote a column titled "Shouts and Murmurs" for *The New Yorker*. His editor at the magazine was quoted as saying, "I guess he was one of the most dreadful writers who ever existed," although the great bookman Vincent Starrett selected his *While Rome Burns* as one of the fifty-two "Best Loved Books of the Twentieth Century."

He was one of the founders of the Algonquin Round Table (just as he later was one of the charter members of the Baker Street Irregulars, famously arriving at the first dinner in a hansom cab). He loved the theater, and with his fellow member George S. Kaufman wrote two plays, both failures. Kaufman, with Moss Hart, later wrote *The Man Who Came to Dinner* and based the titular character, Sheridan Whiteside, on Woollcott, exaggerating his best and worst characteristics. Less well known is that he also served as the inspiration for Waldo Lydecker in the noir film *Laura*. Clifton Webb, who played the columnist, also toured as Whiteside in *The Man Who Came to Dinner;* Woollcott also starred in a traveling company of the comedy. Although he didn't like Los Angeles, calling it "seven suburbs in search of a city," he liked being in films and had numerous small parts and cameos. He died on January 23, 1943.

"All the things I really like to do are either immoral, illegal, or fattening."

—Alexander Woollcott

Moonlight Sonata

by **Alexander Woollcott**

IF THIS REPORT WERE TO BE PUBLISHED in its own England, I would have to cross my fingers in a little foreword explaining that all the characters were fictitious—which stern requirement of the British libel law would embarrass me slightly because none of the characters is fictitious, and the story—told to Katharine Cornell by Clemence Dane and by Katharine Cornell told to me—chronicled what, to the best of my knowledge and belief, actually befell a young English physician whom I shall call Alvan Barach, because that does not happen to be his name. It is an account of a hitherto unreported adventure he had two years ago when he went down into Kent to visit an old friend—let us call him Ellery Cazalet—

who spent most of his days on the links and most of his nights wondering how he would ever pay the death duties on the collapsing family manor-house to which he had indignantly fallen heir.

This house was a shabby little cousin to Compton Wynyates, with roof-tiles of Tudor red making it cozy in the noon-day sun and a hoarse bell which, from the clock tower, had been contemptuously scattering the hours like coins ever since Henry VIII was a rosy stripling. Within, Cazalet could afford only a doddering couple to fend for him, and the once sumptuous gardens did much as they pleased under the care of a single gardener. I think I must risk giving the gardener's real name, for none I could invent would have so appropriate a flavor.

It was John Scripture, and he was assisted, from time to time, by an aged and lunatic father who, in his lucid intervals, would be let out from his captivity under the eaves of the lodge to putter amid the lewd topiarian extravagance of the hedges.

The doctor was to come down when he could, with a promise of some good golf, long nights of exquisite silence, and a ghost or two thrown in—his fancy ran that way. It was a characteristic of his rather ponderous humor that, in writing to fix a day, he addressed Cazalet at *The Creeps, Sevenoaks, Kent.* When he arrived, it was to find his host away from home and not due back until all hours. Barach was to dine alone with a reproachful setter for companion, and not wait up. His bedroom on the ground floor was beautifully paneled from footboard to ceiling, but some misguided housekeeper under the fourth George had fallen upon the lovely woodwork with a can of black varnish. The dowry brought by a Cazalet bride of the mauve decade had been invested in a few vintage bathrooms, and one of these had replaced a prayer closet that once opened into this bedroom. There was only a candle to read by, but the light of a full moon came waveringly through the wind-stirred vines that half-curtained the mullioned windows.

In this museum, Barach dropped off to sleep. He did not know how long he had slept when he found himself awake again, and conscious that something was astir in the room. It took him a moment to place the movement, but at last, in a patch of moonlight, he made out a hunched figure that seemed to be sitting with bent, engrossed head in the chair by the door. It was the hand, or rather the whole arm, that was moving, tracing a recurrent if irregular course in the air. At first, the gesture was teasingly half-familiar, and then Barach recognized it as the one a woman makes when embroidering. There would be a hesitation as if the needle were being thrust through some taut, resistant material, and then, each time, the long, swift, sure pull of the thread.

To the startled guest, this seemed the least menacing activity he had ever heard ascribed to a ghost, but just the same he had only one idea, and that was to get out of that room with all possible dispatch. His mind made a hasty reconnaissance. The door into the hall was out of the question, for madness lay that way. At least he would have to pass right by that weaving arm. Nor did he relish a blind plunge into the thorny shrubbery beneath his window, and a barefoot scamper across the frosty turf. Of course, there was the bathroom, but that was small comfort if he could not get out of it by another door. In a spasm of concentration he remembered that he had seen another door. Just at the moment of this realization, he heard the comfortingly actual sound of a car coming up the drive, and guessed that it was his host returning. In one magnificent movement he leaped to the floor, bounded into the bathroom, and bolted its door behind him. The floor of the room beyond was quilted with moonlight. Wading through that, he arrived breathless, but unmolested, in the corridor. Farther along he could see the lamp left burning in the entrance hall and hear the clatter of his host closing the front door.

As Barach came hurrying out of the darkness to greet him, Cazalet boomed his delight at such affability, and famished by his long, cold ride, proposed an immediate raid on the larder. The doctor, already sheepish at his recent panic, said nothing about it, and was all for food at once. With lighted candles held high, the foraging party descended on the offices, and mine host was descanting on the merits of cold roast beef, Cheddar cheese, and milk as a light midnight snack when he stumbled over a bundle on the floor. With a cheerful curse at the old goody of the kitchen who was always leaving something about, he bent to see what it was this time, and let out a whistle of surprise. Then, by two candles held low, he and the doctor saw something they will not forget while they live. It was the body of the cook. Just the body. The head was gone. On the floor alongside lay a bloody cleaver.

"Old Scripture, by God!" Cazalet cried out, and in a flash Barach guessed. Still clutching a candle in one hand, he dragged his companion back through the interminable house to the room from which he had fled, motioning him to be silent, tiptoeing the final steps. That precaution was wasted, for a regiment could not have disturbed the rapt contentment of the ceremony still in progress within. The old lunatic had not left his seat by the door. Between his knees he still held the head of the woman he had killed. Scrupulously, happily, crooning at his work, he was plucking out the gray hairs one by one.

GEORGE S. KAUFMAN & HOWARD DIETZ

Known as "the gloomy dean of American humor," George Kaufman was born in Pittsburgh, Pennyslvania, on November 16, 1889. He added the "S" to his name "to give it balance," he said. He began his writing career as a journalist and critic, serving as the drama editor of the *New York Times.*

Also known as "the great collaborator," Kaufman worked with many of the greatest names in Broadway history to produce more than forty plays and musicals, including *June Moon* with Ring Lardner, *The Late George Apley* with John P. Marquand, *The Solid Gold Cadillac* with Howard Teichmann, and three collaborations each with Edna Ferber and Marc Connelly. His greatest successes came with Moss Hart, with whom he wrote *Once in a Lifetime, Merrily We Roll Along, You Can't Take It with You,* which won the Pulitzer Prize in 1937, and *The Man Who Came to Dinner.* With Morrie Ryskind and George and Ira Gershwin, he wrote *Of Thee I Sing,* which became the first musical to win a Pulitzer Prize, and *Strike Up the Band.* He also wrote such plays and movies for the Marx Brothers as *Animal Crackers, The Cocoanuts,* and *A Night at the Opera.* He died in New York on June 2, 1961.

Howard Dietz (1896–1983) is a member of the Songwriters Hall of Fame for having written the lyrics to such standards as "Dancing in the Dark," "That's Entertainment," and "You and the Night and the Music." He collaborated with his longtime partner, Arthur Schwartz, writing the book and lyrics for a dozen Broadway shows, including *The Band Wagon.* As an executive at MGM, he is credited with creating its famous logo of Leo the Lion and its motto, *ars gratia artis* (art for art's sake).

The Great Warburton Mystery was first produced in 1931.

Suggesting his own epitaph: "Over my dead body."

—**George S. Kaufman**

The Great Warburton Mystery

by **George S. Kaufman and Howard Dietz**

FIRST PRODUCED IN THE REVUE *The Band Wagon*, at the New Amsterdam Theater, on June 3, 1931, with the following cast:

IVY MEREDITH . . . . ADELE ASTAIRE
INSPECTOR CARTWRIGHT . . FRANK MORGAN
MRS. BOULE . . . . HELEN CARRINGTON
MR. BOULE . . . . ED JEROME
MISS HUTTON . . . . ROBERTA ROBINSON
MR. DODD . . . . PETER CHAMBERS
MR. WALLACE . . . . JOHN BAKER
WALKER . . . . PHILIP LOEB
FIRST POLICEMAN . . . . JAY WILSON
SECOND POLICEMAN . . . . LEON ALTON
THE MURDERED MAN . . . . FRANCES PIBRIOT

SCENE: *The library in the house of Hugh Warburton.* MR. WARBURTON, *who has been killed before the curtain rises, is found slumped in a chair. On the table beside him is a wine glass, almost empty, together with the revolver with which he has obviously been shot. On the other side of the table is another chair—an easy chair, and so turned that it seems likely that the murderer had been sitting in this chair just before, or perhaps when, he fired the fatal shot. Several men and women, all in evening clothes, stand around in various attitudes of shock and discomfort. In the main they are clustered together at the right side of the stage, as though they had entered the room together and remained almost in a frozen group. Standing near the group, but a bit apart from them, is a butler, named* WALKER. *Also present are two policemen—one of whom stands near the body of the dead man and seems to be in general charge. The other is on guard at the left door.*

MRS. BOULE: I tell you I can't stand it!

MISS HUTTON: And neither can I!

MR. BOULE: (*To the* POLICEMEN) Surely something can be done about this. My wife is very nervous. Can't the women go into the other room?

DODD: Yes!

FIRST POLICEMAN: Sorry, sir. No one is allowed to leave until the Inspector comes.

DODD: But when's he going to get here?

FIRST POLICEMAN: He'll be here any minute, sir.

WALLACE: Any minute . . .

MR. BOULE: It's an outrage!

MISS HUTTON: Good heavens.

IVY: (*Detaching herself from the group*) Well, while we're waiting, who wants to shoot a little crap?

MR. BOULE: Ivy!

IVY: Sorry.

(*The door bell rings*)

MR. BOULE: Here he is!

DODD: At last!

MRS. BOULE: Do you think we can go home now?

MR. BOULE: The Inspector will tell us.

MISS HUTTON: The whole thing is an outrage!

SECOND POLICEMAN: Right in here, sir.

BOULE: Here he is now!

WALLACE: This is our man.

MRS. BOULE: And about time.

(*Enter* INSPECTOR CARTWRIGHT. *A quick look around, his gaze lands on* WALKER, *who is standing just inside the door.*)

CARTWRIGHT: Is this the dead man?

FIRST POLICEMAN: No, here, sir.

CARTWRIGHT: Oh. (*He crosses and examines body*) When did this happen?

FIRST POLICEMAN: About eight o'clock, sir.

CARTWRIGHT: How long have you been here?

FIRST POLICEMAN: (*Looking at watch*) Twenty minutes, sir.

CARTWRIGHT: Has he been touched?

FIRST POLICEMAN: No, sir.

CARTWRIGHT: (*A brisk nod; another look around; faces the group*) Good evening. (*There is a scattered response*) My name is Cartwright. Inspector, First District. (*Responses from guests*)

IVY: (*Approaching brightly*) I'm Ivy Meredith. We've had a little trouble here—

CARTWRIGHT: (*Shutting her up*) Good evening.

IVY: (*Taken aback*) Oh, the hell with you.

CARTWRIGHT: Now then, tell me what happened.

MR. BOULE: We were sitting in the D.R.

MRS. BOULE: There's been a man murdered.

WALLACE: I don't know anything about it.

(*Several guests start to reply*)

CARTWRIGHT: If you please—I would like to hear from the officer.

FIRST POLICEMAN: Well, sir, the late gentlemen here was giving a dinner. The dining room is in there. And, after it was over, the men were sitting in there drinking. The women had gone upstairs.

IVY: If you please!

FIRST POLICEMAN: Mr. Warburton said he wanted to get something and came in here.

MR. BOULE: That's right.

FIRST POLICEMAN: He brought the wine glass with him.

CARTWRIGHT: I see.

FIRST POLICEMAN: A minute later there was a shot, and they found him here.

CARTWRIGHT: Who found him here?

FIRST POLICEMAN: All of them, sir.

MR. BOULE: All of us.

FIRST POLICEMAN: The men came in from the dining room, and the women came downstairs.

CARTWRIGHT: But one of them *might* have come down before that?

FIRST POLICEMAN: Yes, sir.

CARTWRIGHT: And gone up again?

FIRST POLICEMAN: Yes, sir.

CARTWRIGHT: Or one of them men might have left the dining room?

FIRST POLICEMAN: Yes, sir.

IVY: I wouldn't have a mind like that—

CARTWRIGHT: Whose gun is it?

FIRST POLICEMAN: His own, sir. It was on the wall.

CARTWRIGHT: His own, eh? So it might have been—anyone.

FIRST POLICEMAN: Yes, sir. Anyone.

IVY: Maybe we'd better send for the police.

(CARTWRIGHT *stands beside chair; reaches toward gun; pretends to point it at dead man's head. Tries same thing from other side*)

FIRST POLICEMAN: Sir?

CARTWRIGHT: It can't be done from either side of the chair. The gun was fired from this angle. (*He draws an imaginary line that cuts squarely across the chair*)

FIRST POLICEMAN: That's right, sir.

CARTWRIGHT: He might have stood back of the chair. But he never would have put the gun over there, because he couldn't reach it.

WALLACE: That's what he couldn't.

DODD: No.

MR. BOULE: He's right.

FIRST POLICEMAN: Maybe he sat in the chair, sir.

CARTWRIGHT: Exactly.

MR. BOULE: That's it.

WALLACE: He sat in the chair.

DODD: That's what he did.

CARTWRIGHT: (*Tries it, but does not actually sit*) He sat in the chair. Perfect for the gun. (*Illustrating*) Perfect for the bullet hole.

IVY: Marvelous for the bullet hole.

CARTWRIGHT: (*Straightens up; looks at chair*) He sat in the chair. (*The phrase runs through the crowd, in little hushed whispers*) No one has left this house since the murder was committed?

FIRST POLICEMAN: No, sir.

CARTWRIGHT: You're positive?

FIRST POLICEMAN: Yes, sir.

CARTWRIGHT: (*A second thought*) You can take the body out. Have this office stand guard until further notice. (*The* POLICEMEN *pick it up; there are expressions of relief from several of the women*) I shall ask the ladies to step to this side of the room. If any of you are faint, you may sit down. (IVY *moves to sit in the fatal chair*) Not there, please. *(The* POLICEMEN, *having removed the body, return as soon as possible*) Ladies and gentlemen, no one has left this house since the murder was committed. I regret very much to inform you that the guilty person is in this room.

MRS. BOULE: Good heavens!

MISS HUTTON: What?

MR. BOULE: Do you mean to insinuate—

CARTWRIGHT: Not at all, sir. I am simply announcing a fact. Someone in this room had a motive for killing H. W. Perhaps a business quarrel. Possibly—who can tell—(*Turning to the women*) some woman he had wronged. (*All four women drop their bags*) Ladies and gentlemen, there can be no guesswork in modern crime detection. It is a matter of cold science. The man or woman who killed Hugh Warburton sat in this chair. No two people in the world, upon sitting in a chair, leave exactly the same impression.

(IVY *looks at cushion*)

DODD: What did he say?

WALLACE: What's he trying to get at?

MR. BOULE: Search me.

CARTWRIGHT: Ladies and gentlemen, the murderer of Hugh Warburton has left his calling card on that cushion, just as plainly as if he had written his name.

DODD: Oh, come now.

WALLACE: What?

MR. BOULE: Absurd!

CARTWRIGHT: On the contrary, a scientific fact. Find the person who fits that cushion, and you will have the murderer of Hugh Warburton.

MISS HUTTON: Good heavens!

MR. BOULE: I don't believe it!

DODD: What an idea!

WALLACE: It's not true!

CARTWRIGHT: But it is true! There are no two exactly alike in the world.

MR. BOULE: Now, really!

IVY: (*After a moment's pause*) I don't know—it's kind of a comfort.

MR. BOULE: What!

IVY: You wouldn't want to have one just like somebody else's.

CARTWRIGHT: And now, with your kind permission, ladies and gentlemen, we will proceed with the examination.

IVY: You will do what?

CARTWRIGHT: I will ask you all to take your places in line, please. Officer!

FIRST POLICEMAN: All right—line up, please! Line right up!

MR. BOULE: This is an outrage!

IVY: It certainly is.

CARTWRIGHT: I regret very much that I must ask you to do this—

IVY: You don't regret it at all, you probably get a great kick out of it.

CARTWRIGHT: Are we ready?

DODD: Well, I suppose if we must we must.

(CARTWRIGHT *takes out a tape measure; unrolls it with a little zipping sound. He looks at the line, which is facing the audience. He measures the print in the chair, then looks up again. He considers—shall he ask the line to turn around or not? Finally decides to take a trip around the back; goes accompanied by the two* POLICEMEN. *He conducts his inspection; each person tries to act unconcerned as he or she is reached*)

IVY: (*As he comes down the line,* CARTWRIGHT *comes to her. She sings a bit of song to show her unconcern*) Are you looking for something?

CARTWRIGHT: (*In a low voice, to a* POLICEMAN) Sixty-two.

IVY: You mean across?

CARTWRIGHT: Never mind, madam. (*Clears his throat; comes in front of the line again*) Ladies and gentlemen, there is only one which—interests me—(*To* IVY) I'm sorry to inform you, madam, that—it belongs to you.

IVY: Me?

CARTWRIGHT: That is right.

IVY: What do you want to do now—make a bust of it?

CARTWRIGHT: Officer, will you bring down that chair please.

IVY: You mean you're going to take an impression?

CARTWRIGHT: (*Bowing*) That's the size of it.

IVY: What's the size of it?

CARTWRIGHT: (*Moves to a spot beside the fatal chair*) Won't you—sit down? (*She hesitates*) If the shoe does not fit—I beg your pardon—then I shall have to admit my mistake.

(*With great dignity she advances to the cushion. Somewhat timidly, she sits. Bounces immediately up again.* CARTWRIGHT *peers quickly: the others strain to see*)

MR. BOULE: Well?

CARTWRIGHT: (*A tense moment*) No. (*A general sigh*) I seem to have been wrong. There's nobody else in the house?

FIRST POLICEMAN: Only a cook, sir. The kitchen's in the cellar—she couldn't possibly get up.

CARTWRIGHT: (*A long sigh. Takes handkerchief in hand and picks up the gun. Shakes his head; puts it down. Takes up the wine glass; regards it*) You men who were in the dining room with him—do you remember if this glass was full when he left the room?

DODD: I think it was.

MR. BOULE: I'd just filled it.

CARTWRIGHT: It would have taken him at least a minute to drink it.

WALKER: Not quite that long, sir.

CARTWRIGHT: What?

WALKER: The glass doesn't hold very much, sir. It has a false bottom.

CARTWRIGHT: Ah! A false bottom.

WALKER: Yes, sir.

CARTWRIGHT: A false bottom. (*Something about the way that he says it makes* WALKER *suspicious. He makes a bolt for it*) Catch him, you men! (*The* POLICEMEN *grab him.* CARTWRIGHT *strides over and pulls a pillow out of the rear of his trousers*) I thought so. Aha! Put him down there! (*The* POLICEMEN *get him on the cushion; pull him up.* CARTWRIGHT *quickly compares the print*) Exactly! There is your man, Officer! Arrest him!

WALKER: I'm glad I did it! He wronged my sister!

IVY: (*Looking at the print*) Good heavens! (*Cries from the guests—"What is it?" "What's the trouble?" etc.*) He's my father! (*To* WALKER) Daddy!

BLACKOUT

Dorothy Parker

Born Dorothy Rothschild in Long Beach, New Jersey, on August 22, 1893, the poet and humorist joked that she got married only to escape her name, keeping her husband's name after they divorced. Soon after being named drama critic for *Vanity Fair* in 1919, filling in for the vacationing P. G. Wodehouse, she helped form the Algonquin Round Table by lunching with her new friends Robert Benchley and Robert Sherwood.

Famous for her vicious wit, she was fired from *Vanity Fair* in 1920 after offending too many people. Benchley and Sherwood resigned in protest. She then worked for *The New Yorker* and published several volumes of poems and short stories before moving to Hollywood with her new husband, Alan Campbell, where she enjoyed great success for fifteen years, including receiving an Academy Award nomination for the screenplay of *A Star Is Born;* she also made script additions to Alfred Hitchcock's *Saboteur.*

In her later years, she became increasingly active in left-wing causes, even describing herself as a communist (though she never joined the party). Her vocal support of communism got her placed on the blacklist by the heads of Hollywood studios. She died of a heart attack in New York at the age of 73 on June 7, 1967, having survived numerous failed suicide attempts for fifty years.

Writing about a Yale prom night: "If all those sweet young things present were laid end to end, I wouldn't be at all surprised."

—**Dorothy Parker**

Big Blonde

by **Dorothy Parker**

HAZEL MORSE WAS A LARGE, FAIR WOMAN of the type that incites some men when they use the word "blonde" to click their tongues and wag their heads roguishly. She prided herself upon her small feet and suffered for her vanity, boxing them in snub-toed, high-heeled slippers of the shortest bearable size. The curious things about her were her hands, strange terminations to the flabby white arms splattered with pale tan spots—long, quivering hands with deep and convex nails. She should not have disfigured them with little jewels.

She was not a woman given to recollections. At her middle thirties, her old days were a blurred and flickering sequence, an imperfect film, dealing with the actions of strangers.

In her twenties, after the deferred death of a hazy widowed mother, she had been employed as a model in a wholesale dress establishment—it was still the day of the big woman, and she was then prettily colored and erect and high-breasted. Her job was not onerous, and she met numbers of men and spent numbers of evenings with them, laughing at their jokes and telling them she loved their neckties. Men liked her, and she took it for granted that the liking of many men was a desirable thing. Popularity seemed to her to be worth all the work that had to be put into its achievement. Men liked you because you were fun, and when they liked you they took you out, and there you were. So, and successfully, she was fun. She was a good sport. Men like a good sport.

No other form of diversion, simpler or more complicated, drew her attention. She never pondered if she might not be better occupied doing something else. Her ideas, or, better, her acceptances, ran right along, with those of the other substantially built blondes in whom she found her friends.

When she had been working in the dress establishment some years she met Herbie Morse. He was thin, quick, attractive, with shifting lines about his shiny, brown eyes and a habit of fiercely biting at the skin around his finger nails. He drank largely; she found that entertaining. Her habitual greeting to him was an allusion to his state of the previous night.

"Oh, what a peach you had," she used to say, through her easy laugh. "I thought I'd die, the way you kept asking the waiter to dance with you."

She liked him immediately upon their meeting. She was enormously amused at his fast, slurred sentences, his interpolations of apt phrases from vaudeville acts and comic strips; she thrilled at the feel of his lean arm tucked firm beneath the sleeve of her coat; she wanted to touch the wet, flat surface of his hair. He was as promptly drawn to her. They were married six weeks after they had met.

She was delighted at the idea of being a bride; coquetted with it, played upon it. Other offers of marriage she had had, and not a few of them, but it happened that they were all from stout, serious men who had visited the dress establishment as buyers; men from Des Moines and Houston and Chicago and, in her phrase, even funnier places. There was always something immensely comic to her in the thought of living elsewhere than New York. She could not regard as serious proposals that she share a western residence.

She wanted to be married. She was nearing thirty now, and she did not take the years well. She spread and softened, and her darkening hair turned her to inexpert dabblings with peroxide. There were times when she had little flashes of fear about her job. And she had had a couple of thousand evenings of being a good sport among her male acquaintances. She had come to be more conscientious than spontaneous about it.

Herbie earned enough, and they took a little apartment far uptown. There was a Mission-furnished dining-room with a hanging central light globed in liver-colored glass; in the living-room were an "overstuffed suite," a Boston fern, and a reproduction of the Henner "Magdalene" with the red hair and the blue draperies; the bedroom was in gray enamel and old rose, with Herbie's photograph on Hazel's dressing-table and Hazel's likeness on Herbie's chest of drawers.

She cooked—and she was a good cook—and marketed and chatted with the delivery boys and the colored laundress. She loved the flat, she loved her life, she loved Herbie. In the first months of their marriage, she gave him all the passion she was ever to know.

She had not realized how tired she was. It was a delight, a new game, a holiday, to give up being a good sport. If her head ached or her arches throbbed, she complained piteously, babyishly. If her mood was quiet, she did not talk. If tears came to her eyes, she let them fall.

She fell readily into the habit of tears during the first

year of her marriage. Even in her good sport days, she had been known to weep lavishly and disinterestedly on occasion. Her behavior at the theater was a standing joke. She could weep at anything in a play—tiny garments, love both unrequited and mutual, seduction, purity, faithful servitors, wedlock, the triangle.

"There goes Haze," her friends would say, watching her. "She's off again."

Wedded and relaxed, she poured her tears freely. To her who had laughed so much, crying was delicious. All sorrows became her sorrows; she was Tenderness. She would cry long and softly over newspaper accounts of kidnaped babies, deserted wives, unemployed men, strayed cats, heroic dogs. Even when the paper was no longer before her, her mind revolved upon these things and the drops slipped rhythmically over her plump cheeks.

"Honestly," she would say to Herbie, "all the sadness there is in the world when you stop to think about it!"

"Yeah," Herbie would say.

She missed nobody. The old crowd, the people who brought her and Herbie together, dropped from their lives, lingeringly at first. When she thought of this at all, it was only to consider it fitting. This was marriage. This was peace.

But the thing was that Herbie was not amused.

For a time, he had enjoyed being alone with her. He found the voluntary isolation novel and sweet. Then it palled with a ferocious suddenness. It was as if one night, sitting with her in the steam-heated living-room, he would ask no more; and the next night he was through and done with the whole thing.

He became annoyed by her misty melancholies. At first, when he came home to find her softly tired and moody, he kissed her neck and patted her shoulder and begged her to tell her Herbie what was wrong. She loved that. But time slid by, and he found that there was never anything really, personally, the matter.

"Ah, for God's sake," he would say. "Crabbing again. All right, sit here and crab your head off. I'm going out."

And he would slam out of the flat and come back late and drunk.

She was completely bewildered by what happened to their marriage. First they were lovers; and then, it seemed without transition, they were enemies. She never understood it.

There were longer and longer intervals between his leaving his office and his arrival at the apartment. She went through agonies of picturing him run over and bleeding, dead and covered with a sheet. Then she lost her fears for his safety and grew sullen and wounded. When a person wanted to be with a person, he came as soon as possible. She desperately wanted him to want to be with her; her own hours only marked the time till he would come. It was often nearly nine o'clock before he came home to dinner. Always he had had many drinks, and their effect would die in him, leaving him loud and querulous and bristling for affronts.

He was too nervous, he said, to sit and do nothing for an evening. He boasted, probably not in all truth, that he had never read a book in his life.

"What am I expected to do—sit around this dump on my tail all night?" he would ask, rhetorically. And again he would slam out.

She did not know what to do. She could not manage him. She could not meet him.

She fought him furiously. A terrific domesticity had come upon her, and she would bite and scratch to guard it. She wanted what she called "a nice home." She wanted a sober, tender husband, prompt at dinner, punctual at work. She wanted sweet, comforting evenings. The idea of intimacy with other men was terrible to her; the thought that Herbie might be seeking entertainment in other women set her frantic.

It seemed to her that almost everything she read—novels from the drug-store lending library, magazine stories, women's pages in the papers—dealt with wives who lost their husbands' love. She could bear those, at that, better than accounts of neat, companionable marriage and living happily ever after.

She was frightened. Several times when Herbie came home in the evening, he found her determinedly dressed—she had had to alter those of her clothes that were not new, to make them fasten—and rouged.

"Let's go wild tonight, what do you say?" she would hail him. "A person's got lots of time to hang around and do nothing when they're dead."

So they would go out, to chop houses and the less expensive cabarets. But it turned out badly. She could no longer find amusement in watching Herbie drink. She could not laugh at his whimsicalities, she was so tensely counting his indulgences. And she was unable to keep back her remonstrances—"Ah, come on, Herb, you've had enough, haven't you? You'll feel something terrible in the morning."

He would be immediately enraged. All right, crab; crab, crab, crab, crab, that was all she ever did. What a lousy sport *she* was! There would be scenes, and one or the other of them would rise and stalk out in fury.

She could not recall the definite day that she started drinking, herself. There was nothing separate about her days. Like drops upon a window-pane, they ran together and trickled away. She had been married six months; then a year; then three years.

She had never needed to drink, formerly. She could sit for most of a night at a table where the others were imbibing earnestly and never droop in looks or spirits nor be bored by the doings of those about her. If she took a cocktail, it was so unusual as to cause twenty minutes or so of jocular comment. But now anguish was in her. Frequently, after a quarrel, Herbie would stay out for the night, and she could not learn from him where the time had been spent. Her heart felt tight and sore in her breast, and her mind turned like an electric fan.

She hated the taste of liquor. Gin, plain or in mixtures, made her promptly sick. After experiment, she found that Scotch whisky was best for her. She took it without water, because that was the quickest way to its effect.

Herbie pressed it on her. He was glad to see her drink. They both felt it might restore her high spirits, and their good times together might again be possible.

" 'Atta girl," he would approve her. "Let's see you get boiled, baby."

But it brought them no nearer. When she drank with him, there would be a little while of gaiety and then, strangely without beginning, they would be in a wild quarrel. They would wake in the morning not sure what it had all been about, foggy as to what had been said and done, but each deeply injured and bitterly resentful. There would be days of vengeful silence.

There had been a time when they had made up their quarrels, usually in bed. There would be kisses and little names and assurances of fresh starts. . . . "Oh, it's going to be great now, Herb. We'll have swell times. I was a crab. I guess I must have been tired. But everything's going to be swell. You'll see."

Now there were no gentle reconciliations. They resumed friendly relations only in the brief magnanimity caused by liquor, before more liquor drew them into new battles. The scenes became more violent. There were shouted invectives and pushes, and sometimes sharp slaps. Once she had a black eye. Herbie was horrified next day at sight of it. He did not go to work; he followed her about, suggesting remedies and heaping dark blame on himself. But after they had had a few drinks—"to pull themselves together"—she made so many wistful references to her bruise that he shouted at her and rushed out and was gone for two days.

Each time he left the place in a rage, he threatened never to come back. She did not believe him, nor did she consider separation. Somewhere in her head or her heart was the lazy, nebulous hope that things would change and she and Herbie settle suddenly into soothing married life. Here were her home, her furniture, her husband, her station. She summoned no alternatives.

She could no longer bustle and potter. She had no more vicarious tears; the hot drops she shed were for herself. She walked ceaselessly about the rooms, her thoughts running mechanically round and round Herbie. In those days began the hatred of being alone that she was never to overcome. You could be by yourself when things were all right, but when you were blue you got the howling horrors.

She commenced drinking alone, little, short drinks all through the day. It was only with Herbie that alcohol made her nervous and quick in offense. Alone, it blurred sharp things for her. She lived in a haze of it. Her life took on a dream-like quality. Nothing was astonishing. A Mrs. Martin moved into the flat across the hall. She was a great blonde woman of forty, a promise in looks of what Mrs. Morse was to be. They made acquaintance, quickly became inseparable. Mrs. Morse spent her days in the opposite apartment. They drank together, to brace themselves after the drinks of the nights before.

She never confided her troubles about Herbie to Mrs. Martin. The subject was too bewildering to her to find comfort in talk. She let it be assumed that her husband's business kept him much away. It was not regarded as important; husbands, as such, played but shadowy parts in Mrs. Martin's circle.

Mrs. Martin had no visible spouse; you were left to decide for yourself whether he was or was not dead. She had an admirer, Joe, who came to see her almost nightly. Often he brought several friends with him—"The Boys," they were called. The Boys were big, red, good-humored men, perhaps forty-five, perhaps fifty. Mrs. Morse was glad of invitations to join the parties—Herbie was scarcely ever at home at night now. If he did come home, she did not visit Mrs. Martin. An evening alone with Herbie meant inevitably a quarrel, yet she would stay with him. There was always her thin and wordless idea that, maybe, this night, things would begin to be all right.

The Boys brought plenty of liquor along with them whenever they came to Mrs. Martin's. Drinking with them, Mrs. Morse became lively and good-natured and audacious. She was quickly popular. When she had drunk enough to cloud her most recent battle with Herbie, she was excited by their approbation. Crab, was she? Rotten sport, was she? Well, there were some that thought different.

Ed was one of The Boys. He lived in Utica—had "his own business" there, was the awed report—but he came to New York almost every week. He was married.

He showed Mrs. Morse the then current photographs of Junior and Sister, and she praised them abundantly and sincerely. Soon it was accepted by the others that Ed was her particular friend.

He staked her when they all played poker; sat next her and occasionally rubbed his knee against hers during the game. She was rather lucky. Frequently she went home with a twenty-dollar bill or a ten-dollar bill or a handful of crumpled dollars. She was glad of them. Herbie was getting, in her words, something awful about money. To ask him for it brought an instant row.

"What the hell do you do with it?" he would say, "Shoot it all on Scotch?"

"I try to run this house half-way decent," she would retort. "Never thought of that, did you? Oh, no, his lordship couldn't be bothered with that."

Again, she could not find a definite day, to fix the beginning of Ed's proprietorship. It became his custom to kiss her on the mouth when he came in, as well as for farewell, and he gave her little quick kisses of approval all through the evening. She liked this rather more than she disliked it. She never thought of his kisses when she was not with him.

He would run his hand lingeringly over her back and shoulders.

"Some dizzy blonde, eh?" he would say. "Some doll."

One afternoon she came home from Mrs. Martin's to find Herbie in the bedroom. He had been away for several nights, evidently on a prolonged drinking bout. His face was gray, his hands jerked as if they were on wires. On the bed were two old suitcases, packed high. Only her photograph remained on his bureau, and the wide doors of his closet disclosed nothing but coat-hangers.

"I'm blowing," he said. "I'm through with the whole works. I got a job in Detroit."

She sat down on the edge of the bed. She had drunk much the night before, and the four Scotches she had had with Mrs. Martin had only increased her fogginess.

"Good job?" she said.

"Oh, yeah," he said. "Looks all right."

He closed a suitcase with difficulty, swearing at it in whispers.

"There's some dough in the bank," he said. "The bank book's in your top drawer. You can have the furniture and stuff."

He looked at her, and his forehead twitched.

"God damn it, I'm through, I'm telling you," he cried. "I'm through."

"All right, all right," she said. "I heard you, didn't I?"

She saw him as if he were at one end of a cannon and she at the other. Her head was beginning to ache bumpingly, and her voice had a dreary, tiresome tone. She could not have raised it.

"Like a drink before you go?" she asked.

Again he looked at her, and a corner of his mouth jerked up.

"Cockeyed again for a change, aren't you?" he said. "That's nice. Sure, get a couple of shots, will you?"

She went to the pantry, mixed him a stiff highball, poured herself a couple of inches of whisky and drank it. Then she gave herself another portion and brought the glasses into the bedroom. He had strapped both suitcases and had put on his hat and overcoat. He took his highball.

"Well," he said, and he gave a sudden, uncertain laugh. "Here's mud in your eye."

"Mud in your eye," she said.

They drank. He put down his glass and took up the heavy suitcases.

"Got to get a train around six," he said.

She followed him down the hall. There was a song, a song that Mrs. Martin played doggedly on the phonograph, running loudly through her mind. She had never liked the thing.

"Night and daytime,
Always playtime.
Ain't we got fun?"

At the door he put down the bags and faced her.

"Well," he said. "Well, take care of yourself. You'll be all right, will you?"

"Oh, sure," she said.

He opened the door, then came back to her, holding out his hand.

" 'By, Haze," he said. "Good luck to you."

She took his hand and shook it.

"Pardon my wet glove," she said.

When the door had closed behind him, she went back to the pantry.

She was flushed and lively when she went in to Mrs. Martin's that evening. The Boys were there, Ed among them. He was glad to be in town, frisky and loud and full of jokes. But she spoke quietly to him for a minute.

"Herbie blew today," she said. "Going to live out west."

"That so?" he said. He looked at her and played with the fountain pen clipped to his waistcoat pocket. "Think he's gone for good, do you?" he asked. "Yeah," she said. "I know he is. I know. Yeah."

"You going to live on across the hall just the same?" he said. "Know what you're going to do?"

"Gee, I don't know," she said. "I don't give much of a damn."

"Oh, come on, that's no way to talk," he told her.

"What you need—you need a little snifter. How about it?"

"Yeah," she said. "Just straight."

She won forty-three dollars at poker. When the game broke up, Ed took her back to her apartment.

"Got a little kiss for me?" he asked.

He wrapped her in his big arms and kissed her violently. She was entirely passive. He held her away and looked at her.

"Little tight, honey?" he asked, anxiously. "Not going to be sick, are you?"

"Me?" she said. "I'm swell."

II

When Ed left in the morning, he took her photograph with him. He said he wanted her picture to look at, up in Utica. "You can have that one on the bureau," she said.

She put Herbie's picture in a drawer, out of her sight. When she could look at it, she meant to tear it up. She was fairly successful in keeping her mind from racing around him. Whisky slowed it for her. She was almost peaceful, in her mist.

She accepted her relationship with Ed without question or enthusiasm. When he was away, she seldom thought definitely of him. He was good to her; he gave her frequent presents and a regular allowance. She was even able to save. She did not plan ahead of any day, but her wants were few, and you might as well put money in the bank as have it lying around.

When the lease of her apartment neared its end, it was Ed who suggested moving. His friendship with Mrs. Martin and Joe had become strained over a dispute at poker; a feud was impending.

"Let's get the hell out of here," Ed said. "What I want you to have is a place near the Grand Central. Make it easier for me."

So she took a little flat in the Forties. A colored maid came in every day to clean and to make coffee for her—she was "through with that housekeeping stuff," she said, and Ed, twenty years married to a passionately domestic woman, admired this romantic uselessness and felt doubly a man of the world in abetting it.

The coffee was all she had until she went out to dinner, but alcohol kept her fat. Prohibition she regarded only as a basis for jokes. You could always get all you wanted. She was never noticeably drunk and seldom nearly sober. It required a larger daily allowance to keep her misty-minded. Too little, and she was achingly melancholy.

Ed brought her to Jimmy's. He was proud, with the pride of the transient who would be mistaken for a native, in his knowledge of small, recent restaurants occupying the lower floors of shabby brownstone houses; places where, upon mentioning the name of an habitué friend, might be obtained strange whisky and fresh gin in many of their ramifications. Jimmy's place was the favorite of his acquaintances.

There, through Ed, Mrs. Morse met many men and women, formed quick friendships. The men often took her out when Ed was in Utica. He was proud of her popularity.

She fell into the habit of going to Jimmy's alone when she had no engagement. She was certain to meet some people she knew, and join them. It was a club for her friends, both men and women.

The women at Jimmy's looked remarkably alike, and this was curious, for, through feuds, removals, and opportunities of more profitable contacts, the personnel of the group changed constantly. Yet always the newcomers resembled those whom they replaced. They were all big women and stout, broad of shoulder and abundantly breasted, with faces thickly clothed in soft, high-colored flesh. They laughed loud and often, showing opaque and lusterless teeth like squares of crockery. There was about them the health of the big, yet a slight, unwholesome suggestion of stubborn preservation. They might have been thirty-six or forty-five or anywhere between.

They composed their titles of their own first names with their husbands' surnames—Mrs. Florence Miller, Mrs. Vera Riley, Mrs. Lilian Block. This gave at the same time the solidity of marriage and the glamour of freedom. Yet only one or two were actually divorced. Most of them never referred to their dimmed spouses; some, a shorter time separated, described them in terms of great biological interest. Several were mothers, each of an only child—a boy at school somewhere, or a girl being cared for by a grandmother. Often, well on towards morning, there would be displays of kodak portraits and of tears.

They were comfortable women, cordial and friendly and irrepressibly matronly. Theirs was the quality of ease. Become fatalistic, especially about money matters, they were unworried. Whenever their funds dropped alarmingly, a new donor appeared; this had always happened. The aim of each was to have one man, permanently, to pay all her bills, in return for which she would have immediately given up other admirers and probably would have become exceedingly fond of him; for the affections of all of them were, by now, unexacting, tranquil, and easily arranged. This end, however, grew increasingly difficult yearly. Mrs. Morse was regarded as fortunate.

Ed had a good year, increased her allowance and gave

her a sealskin coat. But she had to be careful of her moods with him. He insisted upon gaiety. He would not listen to admissions of aches or weariness.

"Hey, listen," he would say, "I got worries of my own, and plenty. Nobody wants to hear other people's troubles, sweetie. What you got to do, you got to be a sport and forget it. See? Well, slip us a little smile, then. That's my girl."

She never had enough interest to quarrel with him as she had with Herbie, but she wanted the privilege of occasional admitted sadness. It was strange. The other women she saw did not have to fight their moods. There was Mrs. Florence Miller who got regular crying jags, and the men sought only to cheer and comfort her. The others spent whole evenings in grieved recitals of worries and ills; their escorts paid them deep sympathy. But she was instantly undesirable when she was low in spirits. Once, at Jimmy's, when she could not make herself lively, Ed had walked out and left her.

"Why the hell don't you stay home and not go spoiling everybody's evening?" he had roared.

Even her slightest acquaintances seemed irritated if she were not conspicuously light-hearted.

"What's the matter with you, anyway?" they would say. "Be your age, why don't you? Have a little drink and snap out of it."

When her relationship with Ed had continued nearly three years, he moved to Florida to live. He hated leaving her; he gave her a large check and some shares of a sound stock, and his pale eyes were wet when he said good-by. She did not miss him. He came to New York infrequently, perhaps two or three times a year, and hurried directly from the train to see her. She was always pleased to have him come and never sorry to see him go.

Charley, an acquaintance of Ed's that she had met at Jimmy's, had long admired her. He had always made opportunities of touching her and leaning close to talk to her. He asked repeatedly of all their friends if they had ever heard such a fine laugh as she had. After Ed left, Charley became the main figure in her life. She classified him and spoke of him as "not so bad." There was nearly a year of Charley; then she divided her time between him and Sydney, another frequenter of Jimmy's; then Charley slipped away altogether.

Sydney was a little, brightly dressed, clever Jew. She was perhaps nearest contentment with him. He amused her always; her laughter was not forced.

He admired her completely. Her softness and size delighted him. And he thought she was great, he often told her, because she kept gay and lively when she was drunk.

"Once I had a gal," he said, "used to try and throw

herself out of the window every time she got a can on. Jee-*zuss,*" he added, feelingly.

Then Sydney married a rich and watchful bride, and then there was Billy. No—after Sydney came Ferd, then Billy. In her haze, she never recalled how men entered her life and left it. There were no surprises. She had no thrill at their advent, nor woe at their departure. She seemed to be always able to attract men. There was never another as rich as Ed, but they were all generous to her, in their means.

Once she had news of Herbie. She met Mrs. Martin dining at Jimmy's, and the old friendship was vigorously renewed. The still admiring Joe, while on a business trip, had seen Herbie. He had settled in Chicago, he looked fine, he was living with some woman—seemed to be crazy about her. Mrs. Morse had been drinking vastly that day. She took the news with mild interest, as one hearing of the sex peccadilloes of somebody whose name is, after a moment's groping, familiar.

"Must be damn near seven years since I saw him," she commented. "Gee. Seven years."

More and more, her days lost their individuality. She never knew dates, nor was sure of the day of the week.

"My God, was that a year ago!" she would exclaim, when an event was recalled in conversation.

She was tired so much of the time. Tired and blue.

Almost everything could give her the blues. Those old horses she saw on Sixth Avenue—struggling and slipping along the car-tracks, or standing at the curb, their heads dropped level with their worn knees. The tightly stored tears would squeeze from her eyes as she teetered past on her aching feet in the stubby, champagne-colored slippers.

The thought of death came and stayed with her and lent her a sort of drowsy cheer. It would be nice, nice and restful, to be dead.

There was no settled, shocked moment when she first thought of killing herself; it seemed to her as if the idea had always been with her. She pounced upon all the accounts of suicides in the newspapers. There was an epidemic of self-killings—or maybe it was just that she searched for the stories of them so eagerly that she found many. To read of them roused reassurance in her; she felt a cozy solidarity with the big company of the voluntary dead.

She slept, aided by whisky, till deep into the afternoons, then lay abed, a bottle and glass at her hand, until it was time to dress to go out for dinner. She was beginning to feel towards alcohol a little puzzled distrust, as towards an old friend who has refused a simple favor. Whisky could still soothe her for most of the time, but there were sudden, inexplicable moments when the cloud fell treacherously away from her, and she was sawed by the sorrow and bewilderment and nuisance of all living. She played voluptuously with the thought of cool, sleepy retreat. She had never been troubled by religious belief and no vision of an after-life intimidated her. She dreamed by day of never again putting on tight shoes, of never having to laugh and listen and admire, of never more being a good sport. Never.

But how would you do it? It made her sick to think of jumping from heights. She could not stand a gun. At the theater, if one of the actors drew a revolver, she crammed her fingers into her ears and could not even look at the stage until after the shot had been fired. There was no gas in her flat. She looked long at the bright blue veins in her slim wrists—a cut with a razor blade, and there you'd be. But it would hurt, hurt like hell, and there would be blood to see. Poison—something tasteless and quick and painless—was the thing. But they wouldn't sell it to you in drugstores, because of the law.

She had few other thoughts.

There was a new man now—Art. He was short and fat and exacting and hard on her patience when he was drunk. But there had been only occasionals for some time before him, and she was glad of a little stability. Too, Art must be away for weeks at a stretch, selling silks, and that was restful. She was convincingly gay with him, though the effort shook her.

"The best sport in the world," he would murmur, deep in her neck. "The best sport in the world."

One night, when he had taken her to Jimmy's, she went into the dressing-room with Mrs. Florence Miller. There, while designing curly mouths on their faces with lip-rouge, they compared experiences of insomnia.

"Honestly," Mrs. Morse said, "I wouldn't close an eye if I didn't go to bed full of Scotch. I lie there and toss and turn and toss and turn. Blue! Does a person get blue lying awake that way!"

"Say, listen, Hazel," Mrs. Miller said, impressively, "I'm telling you I'd be awake for a year if I didn't take veronal. That stuff makes you sleep like a fool."

"Isn't it poison, or something?" Mrs. Morse asked.

"Oh, you take too much and you're out for the count," said Mrs. Miller. "I just take five grains—they come in tablets. I'd be scared to fool around with it. But five grains, and you cork off pretty."

"Can you get it anywhere?" Mrs. Morse felt superbly Machiavellian.

"Get all you want in Jersey," said Mrs. Miller. "They won't give it to you here without you have a doctor's prescription. Finished? We'd better go back and see what the boys are doing."

That night, Art left Mrs. Morse at the door of her apartment; his mother was in town. Mrs. Morse was still sober, and it happened that there was no whisky left in her cupboard. She lay in bed, looking up at the black ceiling.

She rose early, for her, and went to New Jersey. She had never taken the tube, and did not understand it. So she went to the Pennsylvania Station and bought a railroad ticket to Newark. She thought of nothing in particular on the trip out. She looked at the uninspired hats of the women about her and gazed through the smeared window at the flat, gritty scene.

In Newark, in the first drug-store she came to, she asked for a tin of talcum powder, a nailbrush, and a box of veronal tablets. The powder and the brush were to make the hypnotic seem also a casual need. The clerk was entirely unconcerned. "We only keep them in bottles," he said, and wrapped up for her a little glass vial containing ten white tablets, stacked one on another.

She went to another drug-store and bought a facecloth, an orange-wood stick, and a bottle of veronal tablets. The clerk was also uninterested.

"Well, I guess I got enough to kill an ox," she thought, and went back to the station.

At home, she put the little vials in the drawer of her dressing-table and stood looking at them with a dreamy tenderness.

"There they are, God bless them," she said, and she kissed her finger-tip and touched each bottle.

The colored maid was busy in the living-room.

"Hey, Nettie." Mrs. Morse called. "Be an angel, will you? Run around to Jimmy's and get me a quart of Scotch."

She hummed while she awaited the girl's return.

During the next few days, whisky ministered to her as tenderly as it had done when she first turned to its aid. Alone, she was soothed and vague, at Jimmy's she was the gayest of the groups. Art was delighted with her. Then, one night, she had an appointment to meet Art at Jimmy's for an early dinner. He was to leave afterward on a business excursion, to be away for a week. Mrs. Morse had been drinking all the afternoon; while she dressed to go out, she felt herself rising pleasurably from drowsiness to high spirits. But as she came out into the street the effects of the whisky deserted her completely, and she was filled with a slow, grinding wretchedness so horrible that she stood swaying on the pavement, unable for a moment to move forward. It was a gray night with spurts of mean, thin snow, and the streets shone with dark ice. As she slowly crossed Sixth Avenue, consciously dragging one foot past the other, a big, scarred horse pulling a rickety express-wagon crashed to his knees before her. The driver swore and screamed and lashed the beast insanely, bringing the whip back over his shoulder for every blow, while the horse struggled to get a footing on the slippery asphalt. A group gathered and watched with interest.

Art was waiting, when Mrs. Morse reached Jimmy's.

"What's the matter with you, for God's sake?" was his greeting to her.

"I saw a horse," she said. "Gee, I—a person feels sorry for horses. I—it isn't just horses. Everything's kind of terrible, isn't it? I can't help getting sunk."

"Ah, sunk, me eye," he said. "What's the idea of all the bellyaching? What have you got to be sunk about?"

"I can't help it," she said.

"Ah, help it, me eye," he said. "Pull yourself together, will you? Come on and sit down, and take that face off you."

She drank industriously and she tried hard, but she could not overcome her melancholy. Others joined them and commented on her gloom, and she could do no more for them than smile weakly. She made little dabs at her eyes with her handkerchief, trying to time her movements so they would be unnoticed, but several times Art caught her and scowled and shifted impatiently in his chair.

When it was time for him to go to his train, she said she would leave, too, and go home.

"And not a bad idea, either," he said. "See if you can't sleep yourself out of it. I'll see you Thursday. For God's sake, try and cheer up by then, will you?"

"Yeah," she said. "I will."

In her bedroom, she undressed with a tense speed wholly unlike her usual slow uncertainty. She put on her nightgown, took off her hair-net and passed the comb quickly through her dry, vari-colored hair. Then she took the two little vials from the drawer and carried them into the bathroom. The splintering misery had gone from her, and she felt the quick excitement of one who is about to receive an anticipated gift.

She uncorked the vials, filled a glass with water and stood before the mirror, a tablet between her fingers. Suddenly she bowed graciously to her reflection, and raised the glass to it.

"Well, here's mud in your eye," she said.

The tablets were unpleasant to take, dry and powdery and sticking obstinately half-way down her throat. It took her a long time to swallow all twenty of them. She stood watching her reflection with deep, impersonal interest, studying the movements of the gulping throat. Once more she spoke aloud.

"For God's sake, try and cheer up by Thursday, will you?" she said. "Well, you know what he can do. He and the whole lot of them."

She had no idea how quickly to expect effect from the veronal. When she had taken the last tablet, she stood uncertainly, wondering, still with a courteous, vicarious interest, if death would strike her down then and there. She felt in no way strange, save for a slight stirring of sickness from the effort of swallowing the tablets, nor did her reflected face look at all different. It would not be immediate, then; it might even take an hour or so.

She stretched her arms high and gave a vast yawn.

"Guess I'll go to bed," she said. "Gee, I'm nearly dead."

That struck her as comic, and she turned out the bathroom light and went in and laid herself down in her bed, chuckling softly all the time.

"Gee, I'm nearly dead," she quoted. "That's a hot one!"

III

Nettie, the colored maid, came in late the next afternoon to clean the apartment, and found Mrs. Morse in her bed. But then, that was not unusual. Usually, though, the sounds of cleaning waked her, and she did not like to wake up. Nettie, an agreeable girl, had learned to move softly about her work.

But when she had done the living-room and stolen in to tidy the little square bedroom, she could not avoid a tiny clatter as she arranged the objects on the dressing-table. Instinctively, she glanced over her shoulder at the sleeper, and without warning a sickly uneasiness crept over her. She came to the bed and stared down at the woman lying there.

Mrs. Morse lay on her back, one flabby, white arm flung up, the wrist against her forehead. Her stiff hair hung untenderly along her face. The bed covers were pushed down, exposing a deep square of soft neck and a pink nightgown, its fabric worn uneven by many launderings; her great breasts, freed from their tight confiner, sagged beneath her arm-pits. Now and then she made knotted, snoring sounds, and from the corner of her opened mouth to the blurred turn of her jaw ran a lane of crusted spittle.

"Mis' Morse," Nettie called. "Oh, Mis' Morse! It's terrible late."

Mrs. Morse made no move.

"Mis' Morse," said Nettie. "Look, Mis' Morse. How'm I goin' get this bed made?"

Panic sprang upon the girl. She shook the woman's hot shoulder.

"Ah, wake up, will yuh?" she whined. "Ah, please wake up."

Suddenly the girl turned and ran out in the hall to the elevator door, keeping her thumb firm on the black, shiny button until the elderly car and its Negro attendant stood before her. She poured a jumble of words over the boy, and led him back to the apartment. He tiptoed creakingly in to the bedside; first gingerly, then so lustily that he left marks in the soft flesh, he prodded the unconscious woman.

"Hey, there!" he cried, and listened intently, as for an echo.

"Jeez. Out like a light," he commented.

At his interest in the spectacle, Nettie's panic left her. Importance was big in both of them. They talked in quick, unfinished whispers, and it was the boy's suggestion that he fetch the young doctor who lived on the ground floor. Nettie hurried along with him. They looked forward to the limelit moment of breaking their news of something untoward, something pleasurably unpleasant. Mrs. Morse had become the medium of drama. With no ill wish to her, they hoped that her state was serious, that she would not let them down by being awake and normal on their return. A little fear of this determined them to make the most, to the doctor, of her present condition. "Matter of life and death," returned to Nettie from her thin store of reading. She considered startling the doctor with the phrase.

The doctor was in and none too pleased at interruption. He wore a yellow and blue striped dressing-gown, and he was lying on his sofa, laughing with a dark girl, her face scaly with inexpensive powder, who perched on the arm.

Half-emptied highball glasses stood beside them, and her coat and hat were neatly hung up with the comfortable implication of a long stay.

Always something, the doctor grumbled. Couldn't let anybody alone after a hard day. But he put some bottles and instruments into a case, changed his dressing-gown for his coat and started out with the Negroes.

"Snap it up there, big boy," the girl called after him. "Don't be all night."

The doctor strode loudly into Mrs. Morse's flat and on to the bedroom, Nettie and the boy right behind him. Mrs. Morse had not moved; her sleep was as deep, but soundless, now. The doctor looked sharply at her, then plunged his thumbs into the lidded pits above her eyeballs and threw his weight upon them. A high, sickened cry broke from Nettie.

"Look like he tryin' to push her right on th'ough the bed," said the boy. He chuckled.

Mrs. Morse gave no sign under the pressure. Abruptly the doctor abandoned it, and with one quick movement swept the covers down to the foot of the bed. With another he flung her nightgown back and lifted the thick, white legs, cross-hatched with blocks of tiny, iris-colored veins. He pinched them repeatedly, with long, cruel nips, back of the knees. She did not awaken.

"What's she been drinking?" he asked Nettie, over his shoulder.

With the certain celerity of one who knows just where to lay hands on a thing, Nettie went into the bathroom, bound for the cupboard where Mrs. Morse kept her whisky. But she stopped at the sight of the two vials, with their red and white labels, lying before the mirror. She brought them to the doctor.

"Oh, for the Lord Almighty's sweet sake!" he said. He dropped Mrs. Morse's legs, and pushed them impatiently across the bed. "What did she want to go taking that tripe for? Rotten yellow trick, that's what a thing like that is. Now we'll have to pump her out, and all that stuff. Nuisance, a thing like that is; that's what it amounts to. Here, George, take me down in the elevator. You wait here, maid. She won't do anything."

"She won't die on me, will she?" cried Nettie.

"No," said the doctor. "God, no. You couldn't kill her with an ax."

IV

After two days, Mrs. Morse came back to consciousness, dazed at first, then with a comprehension that brought with it the slow, saturating wretchedness.

"Oh, Lord, oh, Lord," she moaned, and tears for herself and for life striped her cheeks.

Nettie came in at the sound. For two days she had done the ugly, incessant tasks in the nursing of the unconscious, for two nights she had caught broken bits of sleep on the living-room couch. She looked coldly at the big, blown woman in the bed.

"What you been tryin' to do, Mis' Morse?" she said. "What kine o' work is that, takin' all that stuff?"

"Oh, Lord," moaned Mrs. Morse, again, and she tried to cover her eyes with her arms. But the joints felt stiff and brittle, and she cried out at their ache.

"Tha's no way to ack, takin' them pills," said Nettie. "You can thank you' stars you heah at all. How you feel now?"

"Oh, I feel great," said Mrs. Morse. "Swell, I feel."

Her hot, painful tears fell as if they would never stop.

"Tha's no way to take on, cryin' like that," Nettie said. "After what you done. The doctor, he says he could have you arrested, doin' a thing like that. He was fit to be tied, here."

"Why couldn't he let me alone?" wailed Mrs. Morse. "Why the hell couldn't he have?"

"Tha's terr'ble, Mis' Morse, swearin' an' talkin' like that," said Nettie, "after what people done for you. Here I ain' had no sleep at all for two nights, an' had to give up goin' out to my other ladies!"

"Oh, I'm sorry, Nettie," she said. "You're a peach. I'm

sorry I've given you so much trouble. I couldn't help it. I just got sunk. Didn't you ever feel like doing it? When everything looks just lousy to you?"

"I wouldn' think o' no such thing," declared Nettie. "You got to cheer up. Tha's what you got to do. Everybody's got their troubles."

"Yeah," said Mrs. Morse. "I know."

"Come a pretty picture card for you," Nettie said. "Maybe that will cheer you up."

She handed Mrs. Morse a post-card. Mrs. Morse had to cover one eye with her hand, in order to read the message; her eyes were not yet focusing correctly.

It was from Art. On the back of a view of the Detroit Athletic Club he had written: "Greeting and salutations. Hope you have lost that gloom. Cheer up and don't take any rubber nickles. See you on Thursday."

She dropped the card to the floor. Misery crushed her as if she were between great smooth stones. There passed before her a slow, slow pageant of days spent lying in her flat, of evenings at Jimmy's being a good sport, making herself laugh and coo at Art and other Arts; she saw a long parade of weary horses and shivering beggars and all beaten, driven, stumbling things. Her feet throbbed as if she had crammed them into the stubby champagne-colored slippers. Her heart seemed to swell and harden.

"Nettie," she cried, "for heaven's sake pour me a drink, will you?"

The maid looked doubtful.

"Now you know, Mis' Morse," she said, "you been near daid. I don' know if the doctor he let you drink nothin' yet."

"Oh, never mind him," she said. "You get me one, and bring in the bottle. Take one yourself."

"Well," said Nettie.

She poured them each a drink, deferentially leaving hers in the bathroom to be taken in solitude, and brought Mrs. Morse's glass in to her.

Mrs. Morse looked into the liquor and shuddered back from its odor. Maybe it would help. Maybe, when you had been knocked cold for a few days, your very first drink would give you a lift. Maybe whisky would be her friend again. She prayed without addressing a God, without knowing a God. Oh, please, please, let her be able to get drunk, please keep her always drunk.

She lifted the glass.

"Thanks, Nettie," she said. "Here's mud in your eye."

The maid giggled. "Tha's the way, Mis' Morse," she said. "You cheer up, now."

"Yeah," said Mrs. Morse. "Sure."

Up the Close and Down the Stair

by **S. J. Perelman**

I'M NO BLOODY HERO, and when the Princess Pats stood at Passchendaele in '17, I was damned careful to be twelve years old and three thousand miles to the rear, selling Domes of Silence after school to the housewives of Crescent Park, Rhode Island. I never go out of my way to borrow trouble, but if it comes, I pride myself I can face up to it as well as the average Johnny. I once spent a night in a third-class carriage in the F.M.S. with seventy-odd indentured Chinese out of Swatow and Amoy bound up-country for the tin mines at Ipoh. Blasted engine broke a coupling, way up the back of beyond in Negri Sembilan, and there we sat, rain pelting through the roof, not a cup of tea to be had, and every mother's son of them smoking chandoo and tucking in rice mixed with *trassi,* compared to which even the durian is attar of roses. Worse luck, the coolie in the berth over mine kept munching bananas and dropping the skins on me; half a dozen times, you'd have sworn a cobra or a Russell's viper was loose in your bed. Touch and go, as they say, but I bit on the bullet and the old buckram carried me through. Another time, down Amboina way in the Moluccas, a chap buying *bêche-de-mer* and shell in the Kai and Aru groups southeast of Ceram offered me a lift as far as Banda Neira in his prahu. A filthy scrow she was, thirty-five tons, with a poop deck and double sweeps, manned by a crew of Bugi who'd slip a kris into you at the drop of a diphthong. Well, you know the Banda Sea at the turn of the monsoon, treacherous as a woman, waves thirty feet high one minute and flat calm the next, wind howling like a thousand devils and sharks all over the ruddy place. Thinks I, weighing the beggar's proposal in the bar in Amboina, steady on, old son, better have another drink on it. We'd a second bottle of *genever* and a third, till I could almost feel the eyes start out of my blooming head. Lord knows how I managed to stick it, but she sailed without me and that was the last ever heard of the lot of them. I probably would have heard more, except I had to rush back to New York to see about my Social Security.

Yes, the going has to be pretty rugged before I show the white feather, and when it comes along, I'm willing to own up to it. A couple of weeks ago, business called me up to town from my Pennsylvania retreat and I stayed alone overnight at our flat in Greenwich Village. This much I'll say: I've knocked about a bit and I've taken the rough with the smooth, but I wouldn't duplicate that experience for all the rubies in the Shwe Dagon Pagoda. Just in a manner of speaking, that is. If anybody wants to talk a deal, I can be in Rangoon in two days.

Maybe, since the circumstances were special, I ought to sketch in the background. Last December, deferring to my wife's prejudice against sleeping on subway gratings, I moved the family into a handsome old brownstone on West Ninth Street. It was a charming house, its brick front weathered a soft rose under the ivy, with a cool, spacious stair well and a curving walnut balustrade worn smooth by the hands of many a defaulting tenant. Determined to apportion the charm among the greatest possible number of people, the owner had cut up the premises into eight apartments, and the top floors in particular into two minute duplexes, the rear one of which we invested. It commanded an unbroken view of a health-food shop on Eighth Street, and of a dismal winter afternoon it was heartening to watch the dyspeptics totter out carrying pails of blackstrap molasses and wheat germ, their faces exalted with the gospel of Gayelord Hauser. The services, to be candid, were deplorable. The hot-water taps supplied a brown viscous fluid similar to cocoa, the radiators beat an unending tomtom like the Royal Watusi Drums, and the refrigerator poached our food instead of chilling it, but the mem and I didn't care a fig. We were living graciously; we could breathe. We thanked our lucky stars we weren't cooped up in one of those great uniform apartments on Park Avenue, full of stall showers and gas ranges that work, and all kinds of depressing gadgets.

About a month after moving in, I learned a beguiling fact from another tenant; viz., that three decades before, the house had been the scene of an audacious heist. To recap the affair briefly: One Sunday afternoon in April, 1922, Mr. and Mrs. Frederick Gorsline, the wealthy elderly couple who occupied the mansion, were enjoying a siesta when five yeggs, led by a French highbinder once employed there as relief butler, gained entrance. They overpowered the householders and their staff of eight, locked them in a wine vault in the basement, and fled, bearing gems and silver worth approximately eighty thousand dollars. That the prisoners escaped from the vault alive was due solely to the sangfroid and enterprise of its seventy-three-year-old owner; working in total darkness with a penknife and a ten-cent piece, he succeeded after two hours in loosening the screws that held the combination in place, and opened the door. He then expended seven years and a sizable part of his bundle tracking down the culprits, the last of whom, the ringleader, was apprehended in France and transported to Devil's Island.

I, naturally, lost no time in making a close scrutiny of the vault with a wax taper, or something the man at the hardware store assured me was a wax taper, and convinced myself of the veracity of the story. I even found a dime embedded in a crack in the floor; it was dated 1936, but I filed off the final numerals and worked up a rather effective account of my role in the case, which folks used to clamor for at our parties this past spring. It was funny the way they'd clamor for it, sometimes without even opening their mouths. They'd just stand there and sort of *yearn,* and being host, of course, I'd have to oblige. But all that is by the way. You're clamoring to hear about the night I put in alone there.

Well, I got downtown about six of a Friday evening, pretty well bushed, no engagements on hand. (Curious the way they'd rather stay home and wash their hair than accept a date at the last minute. I never will understand it.) As I say, I was done up and looking forward to a quiet session with Gibbon or Trevelyan, eleven hours of shut-eye, and an early start back to Pennsylvania in the morning. One of our neighbors, a young fellow who poses for those Bronzini neckwear ads of people with their torsos transfixed by a dirk, was loading a portable sewing machine and a nest of salad bowls into the back of his MG.

"Huddo," he said, startled. "I thought you-all had cleared out." I explained my presence and he shuddered. "Too ghastly. Everyone in the house is away. The Cadmuses drove off this minute to their haunt in Bucks. Even Benno Troglodeit's gone to the beach, and you know what an old stick-in-the-mud *he* is."

"Solitude don't make no never-mind to me," I said loftily. "When one's kicked around the far places of the earth as much as I have, he becomes pretty self-sufficient. I recall one time in Trebizond—" The roar of his powerful little engine drowned out the remainder of my sentence, and with a flick of his wrist he was speeding down Ninth Street. Sensational acceleration, those MGs.

I watched him out of sight, then slowly went upstairs. Somehow—I couldn't have said why—a puzzling change of mood had overtaken me, a vague and indescribable malaise. The house, too, seemed to have altered mysteriously; the stair well was nowhere as cool or spacious as it had been in the past. The air smelled stagnant and oppressive, as though it had been filtered through hot plush, and I imagined some unspeakable secret behind each doorway I passed. Fumbling the key into the lock of our apartment, the distorted, waxen faces of Andrew and Abby Borden rose up before me; with a galvanic twitch, I flung open the door, darted inside, and bolted it fast. By the weak rays of light struggling through the drawn Venetian blinds, I took careful stock of the living room, its floor devoid of carpets and the furniture shrouded in dust covers. Nothing appeared amiss, but I decided to double-check. I licked my lips and spoke in a soft, placating tone that made it clear I wouldn't give offense to a dog. "Is anybody home?" I inquired. It goes without saying that had a reply been vouchsafed, I was prepared to drop dead instantly. Satisfied no corporeal intruders were astir, I stole on padded feet upstairs to the bedrooms—trekking through the jungles of southern Siam long ago taught me how to move without disturbing a twig—and made a routine tour of the closets.

Just as I was feeling around gingerly among the topcoats for any unauthorized bodies, the telephone gave a sudden, nerve-shattering peal. I sprang out and flattened myself against the wall near the instrument, every faculty tensed. Something very, very unsavory was afoot; I distinctly remembered having cancelled the service myself a month before. Ought I answer or play for time? Trying to envision the face at the other end, the twisted smile and the narrow, baleful eyes, I felt perspiration ooze from my scalp. Then equilibrium returned; better to know my enemy than succumb to this nameless, creeping horror. I picked up the receiver. "Grand Central Roach Control," I said tonelessly. "Leonard Vesey speaking." There was a watchful pause, and, realizing the full stature of his adversary, the unknown hung up discomfited.

The first round was mine, but from now on my only safety lay in extreme vigilance. With a view toward sharpening my sensibilities to razor edge, I decided to toss off two fingers of brandy neat. A search of the kitchen cupboards failed to elicit any such restorative; I did, however, turn up a can of warm tomato juice whose top I finally breached with an apple corer. Five or six gauze pads soon dried the trifling gash in my wrist, and, stripping down to my shorts (for I was not minded to carry excess poundage if an emergency arose), I opened my Gibbon to the campaigns of Diocletian.

How noble a spirit infuses those stately periods, what sapience and celestial calm! Musing on the paltriness of latter-day historians, I fell into a gentle reverie that must have lasted close to four hours.

Shortly after midnight, I came awake with the ineradicable conviction that I had neglected some vital obligation. I lay rigid, struggling to recapture it, and suddenly it flashed over me. In the hustle and bustle of moving last fall, I had forgotten to tip the janitor of our new quarters at Christmastime. Suppose, for argument's sake, that he had been brooding over the slight. Suppose that his bitterness had developed into a persecution mania that demanded my extinction, that he had seen me enter the house alone tonight, had seized the chance to put me out of the way, and, at this very moment, was tiptoeing stealthily up the stairs, cleaver in hand. I saw myself cruelly dismembered, my head in a hatbox as in "Night Must Fall," my extremities wrapped in burlap and dispersed through a dozen railway checkrooms. Tears of self-pity welled up in my eyes; I was too young to die in such meaningless fashion, victim of a madman's whim. What would become of my brood in Pennsylvania, waiting for the paternal hug and the sweetmeats that never came? I resolved to sell my life as dearly as possible. Grimly rolling up my figurative sleeves, I was about to burrow under the quilt when a muffled clang from below turned me to stone.

In that awful instant, all the details of the Gorsline robbery reverted with diamond clarity, and the whole hideous truth dawned on me. The police, despite their rodomontade, had never really regained the loot; the brains of the mob had hidden it somewhere in the building, and now, after twenty-nine years in the hell of French Guiana, had come back to exhume it and settle old scores. Like Jonathan Small in "The Sign of Four," returning to Pondicherry Lodge from the Andamans to claim the Agra Treasure, he was a beast unchained, and in slamming the door of the vault he was notifying the occupants of the house that their hour had struck. All that remained was the stab of the poisoned thorn and the last convulsive agony. Ten minutes hence, my features frozen in the dreadful *risus sardonicus,* I would be indistinguishable from Bartholomew Sholto. I was a gone coon.

And yet, such is the complexity of the human spirit, and especially one molded in the crucible of the East, not a muscle flickered in my lean cheek. Instead, I was filled with a vast, consuming anger; I was determined to invade the vault and purge society of this loathsome scourge if it meant annihilation. I routed out the wax taper, boldly flung open the door, and decended the stairs with catlike tread. Just as I neared the first-floor landing, a feminine voice, taut with a terrible urgency, drifted up to me from below.

"Put your back into it," it was saying harshly. "We've got to crack it tonight, I tell you." I repressed an involuntary snort of triumph. So that was it; a woman was mixed up in it—indubitably had engineered the entire caper, as I had suspected from the beginning. Pressed close to the balustrade, I worked myself down along it with infinite caution and peered around the stairhead.

The sight that met my eyes was one calculated to unsettle the most magnificent aplomb. Clad in a flowered kimono that ill concealed her generous charms, Mrs. Purdy Woolwine, the first-floor tenant, knelt by a galvanized rubbish can, striving to anchor it to the floor. Her gleaming coiffure was disordered and her face contorted like that of a wrestler in a Japanese print. At her side, a small, sallow man, whom I dimly recognized as Woolwine, had driven a screwdriver under the lid with the aid of a hammer and was desperately trying to prise it off, obviously bent on disposing of a wastebasket heaped high with bottles and fruit rinds. Neither of them was aware of my existence, nor would they ever have discovered it but for an unbearable compulsion to sneeze. As my wild "Kerchow!" rang out, they wheeled convulsively and beheld me, bone-naked in my shorts and taper in hand, agape on the landing. With an eerie screech that shook the Piranesi reproductions off the walls, Mrs. Woolwine half rose and toppled sidewise in a dead faint.

Fantastic how people deliberately misconstrue the most innocent occurrence. Damn my eyes if I wasn't two hours explaining away the affair to those chuckleheads from the Eighth Precinct. They'd got the wind up, don't you see, had to find a scapegoat and all that frightful rot. You'd have thought I was Harvey Hawley Crippen, the way they mucked about with their sobriety tests and their argel-bargel about Peeping Toms and God knows what all. Ah, well, it's over and done with now, thank goodness. I spend most of my time these days down in Pennsylvania, and, come autumn, we'll probably find digs more suited to the family needs. Might even go out East again, between you and me. I've had my fill of gracious living and cocktail kit-kit and hysteroids named Mrs. Purdy Woolwine. I breathe better in some place like Amboina, where nobody asks any questions, where all you need is a twist of cotton around your loins and a pinch of rice, and a man's past is his own.

EDNA FERBER

Born in Kalamazoo, Michigan, on August 15, 1885, Edna Ferber began her writing career as a journalist, first for the *Appleton Daily Crescent,* then the *Milwaukee Journal,* before covering the Republican and Democratic conventions for the United Press Association in 1920. She moved to New York and was welcomed to the Round Table.

She not only enjoyed great critical acclaim, she was also one of the most successful writers of her day—one of the few Round Table novelists whose works are still read today. As well as being a prolific playwright on her own, Ferber, like Marc Connelly, collaborated on several plays with George S. Kaufman, all of which enjoyed spectacular success: *Stage Door* (1926), *The Royal Family* (1927) and *Dinner at Eight* (1932).

Among her voluminous works were such best-selling novels as *So Big* (1924), which won the Pulitzer Prize, *Show Boat* (1926), *Cimarron* (1929), *Come and Get It* (1935), *Saratoga Trunk* (1941), *Giant* (1952), and *Ice Palace* (1958), all of which were made into major Hollywood motion pictures.

Ferber died of cancer in New York on April 16, 1968.

"The Man Who Came Back" was first published in the April 1911 issue of *The American Magazine.*

"Being an old maid is like death by drowning, a really delightful sensation after you cease to struggle."

—Edna Ferber

The Man Who Came Back

by **Edna Ferber**

THERE ARE TWO WAYS OF DOING BATTLE against Disgrace. You may live it down; or you may run away from it and hide. The first method is heart-breaking, but sure. The second cannot be relied upon because of the uncomfortable way Disgrace has of turning up at your heels just when you think you have eluded her in the last town but one.

Ted Terrill did not choose the first method. He had it thrust upon him. After Ted had served his term he came back home to visit his mother's grave, intending to take the next train out. He wore none of the prison pallor that you read about in books, because he had been short-stop on the penitentiary all-star baseball team, and famed for the dexterity with which he could grab up red-hot grounders. The storied lockstep and the clipped hair effect also were missing. The superintendent of Ted's prison had been one of the reform kind.

You never would have picked Ted for a criminal. He had none of those interesting phrenological bumps and depressions that usually are shown to such frank advantage in the Bertillon photographs. Ted had been assistant cashier in the Citizens' National Bank. In a mad moment he had attempted a little sleight-of-hand act in which certain Citizens' National funds were to be transformed into certain glittering shares and back again so quickly that the examiners couldn't follow it with their eyes. But Ted was unaccustomed to these now-you-see-it-and-now-you-don't feats and his hand slipped. The trick dropped to the floor with an awful clatter.

Ted had been a lovable young kid, six feet high, and blond, with a great reputation as a dresser. He had the first yellow plush hat in our town. It sat on his golden head like a halo. The women all liked Ted. Mrs. Dankworth, the dashing widow (why will widows persist in being dashing?), said that he was the only man in our town who knew how to wear a dress suit. The men were forever slapping him on the back and asking him to have a little something. Ted's good looks and his clever tongue and a certain charming Irish way he had with him caused him to be taken up by the smart set. Now, if you've never lived in a small town you will be much amused at the idea of its boasting a smart set. Which proves your ignorance. The small-town smart set is deadly serious about its smartness. It likes to take three-hour runs down to the city to fit a pair of shoes and attend the opera. Its clothes are as well-made, and its scandals as crisp, and its pace as hasty, and its golf club as dull as the clothes, and scandals, and pace, and golf club of its city cousins.

The hasty pace killed Ted. He tried to keep step in a set of young folks whose fathers had made our town. And all the time his pocket-book was yelling, "Whoa!" The young people ran largely to leather-upholstered convertibles and country-club doings and house parties, as small-town younger generations are apt to. When Ted went to high school half the boys in his little clique spent their after-school hours dashing up and down Main Street in their big, glittering cars, sitting slumped down on the middle of their spines in front of the steering wheel, their sleeves rolled up, their hair combed a militant crew-cut. One or the other of them always took Ted along. It is fearfully easy to develop a taste for that kind of thing. As he grew older, the taste took root and became a habit.

Ted came out after serving his term, still handsome,

in spite of all that story-writers may have taught to the contrary. But we'll make this concession to the old tradition. There was a difference. His radiant blondeur was dimmed in some intangible, elusive way. Birdie Callahan, who worked in Ted's mother's kitchen for years, and who had gone back to her old job at the Haley House after her mistress's death, put it sadly, thus:

"He was always th' han'some divil. I used to look forward to ironin' day just for the pleasure of pressin' his fancy shirts for him. I'm that partial to them swell blonds. But I dinnaw, he's changed. Doin' time has taken the edge off his hair an' complexion. Not changed his color, do yuh mind, but dulled it, like a gold ring, or the like, that has tarnished."

Ted was seated in the smoker, with a chip on his shoulder, and a sick horror of encountering someone he knew in his heart, when Joe Haley, of the Haley House, got on at Westport, homeward bound. Joe Haley is the most eligible bachelor in our town, and the slipperiest. He has made the Haley House a gem, so that traveling men will cut half a dozen towns to Sunday there. If he should say, "Jump through this!" to any girl in our town she'd jump and be very glad to do it.

Joe Haley strolled leisurely up the car aisle toward Ted. Ted saw him coming and sat very still, waiting.

"Hello, Ted! How's Ted?" said Joe Haley, casually. And dropped into the adjoining seat without any more fuss.

Ted wet his lips slightly and tried to say something. He had been a breezy talker. But the words would not come. Joe Haley made no effort to cover the situation with a rush of conversation. He did not seem to realize that there was any situation to cover. He champed the end of his cigar and handed one to Ted.

"Well, you've taken your lickin', kid. What you going to do now?"

The rawness of it made Ted wince. "Oh, I don't know," he stammered. "I've got a job half promised in Chicago."

"What doing?"

Ted laughed a short and ugly laugh. "Driving a brewery truck."

Joe Haley tossed his cigar dexterously to the opposite corner of his mouth and squinted thoughtfully along its bulging sides.

"Remember that Wenzel girl that's kept books for me for the last six years? She's leaving in a couple of months to marry a New York guy that travels for ladies' cloaks and suits. After she goes it's nix with the lady book-keepers for me. Not that Minnie isn't a good, straight girl, and honest, but no girl can keep books with one eye on a column of figures and the other on a traveling man in a brown suit and a red necktie, unless she's cross-eyed, and you bet Minnie ain't. The job's yours if you want it. Eighty a month to start on, and board."

"I—can't, Joe. Thanks just the same. I'm going to try to begin all over again, somewhere else, where nobody knows me."

"Oh yes," said Joe. "I knew a fellow that did that. After he came out he grew a beard, and wore eyeglasses, and changed his name. Had a quick, crisp way of talkin', so he cultivated a drawl and went west and started in business. Real estate, I think. Anyway, the second month he was there in walks a fool he used to know and bellows: 'Why, if it ain't Bill! Hello, Bill! I thought you was doing time yet.' That was enough. Ted, you can black your face, and dye your hair, and squint, and some fine day, sooner or later, somebody'll come along and blab the whole thing. And say, the older it gets the worse it sounds when it does come out. Stick around here where you grew up, Ted."

Ted clasped and unclasped his hands uncomfortably. "I can't figure out why you should care how I finish."

"No reason," answered Joe. "Not a darned one. I wasn't ever in love with your ma, like the guy on the stage; and I never owed your pa a cent. So it ain't a guilty conscience. I guess it's just pure cussedness, and a hankerin' for a new investment. I'm curious to know how'll you turn out. You've got the makin's of what the newspapers call a Leading Citizen, even if you did fall down once. If I'd ever had time to get married, which I never will have, a first-class hotel bein' more worry and expense than a Pittsburgh steel magnate's whole harem, I'd have wanted somebody to do the same for my kid. That sounds slushy, but it's straight."

"I don't seem to know how to thank you," began Ted, a little husky as to voice.

"Call around tomorrow morning," interrupted Joe Haley, briskly, "and Minnie Wenzel will show you the ropes. You and her can work together for a couple of months. After then she's leaving to make her underwear, and that. I should think she'd have a bale of it by this time. Been embroidering them shimmy things and lunch cloths back of the desk when she thought I wasn't lookin' for the last six months."

Ted came down next morning at 8 A.M. with his nerve between his teeth and the chip still balanced lightly on his shoulder. Five minutes later Minnie Wenzel knocked it off. When Joe Haley introduced the two jocularly, knowing that they had originally met in the First Reader room, Miss Wenzel acknowledged the introduction icily by lifting her left eyebrow slightly and drawing down the corners of her mouth. Her air of hauteur was a triumph, considering that she was handicapped by black sateen sleevelets.

I wonder how one could best describe Miss Wenzel? There is one of her in every small town. Let me think (business of hand on brow). Well, she always paid $8 for her girdles when most girls in a similar position got theirs for $1.59 in the basement. Nature had been kind to her. The hair that had been a muddy brown in Minnie's schoolgirl days it had touched with a magic red-gold wand. Birdie Callahan always said that Minnie was working only to wear out her old clothes.

After the introduction Miss Wenzel followed Joe Haley into the lobby. She took no pains to lower her voice.

"Well, I must say, Mr. Haley, you've got a fine nerve! If my gentleman friend was to hear of my working with an ex-con I wouldn't be surprised if he'd break off the engagement. I should think you'd have some respect for the feelings of a lady with a name to keep up, and engaged to a swell fellow like Mr. Stone."

"Say, listen, m' girl," replied Joe Haley. "The law don't cover all the tricks. But if stuffing an order was a criminal offense I'll bet your swell travling man would be doing a life term."

Ted worked that day with his teeth set so that his jaws ached next morning. Minnie Wenzel spoke to him only when necessary and then in terms of dollars and cents. When dinner-time came she divested herself of the black sateen sleevelets and disappeared in the direction of the washroom. Ted waited until the dining-room was almost deserted. Then he went in to dinner alone. Someone in white wearing an absurd little pocket handkerchief of an apron led him to a seat in a far corner of the big room. Ted did not lift his eyes higher than the snowy square of the apron. The Apron drew out a chair, shoved it under Ted's knees in the way Aprons have, and thrust a printed menu at him.

"Roast beef, medium," said Ted, without looking up.

"Bless your heart, yuh ain't changed a bit. I remember how yuh used to jaw when it was too well done," said the Apron, fondly.

Ted's head came up with a jerk.

"So yuh will cut yer old friends, is it?" grinned Birdie Callahan. "If this wasn't a public dining-room maybe yuh'd shake hands with a poor but proud workin' girrul. Yer as good-lookin' a divil as ever, Mister Ted."

Ted's hand shot out and grasped hers. "Birdie! I could weep on your apron! I never was so glad to see anyone in my life. Just to look at you makes me homesick. What in Sam Hill are you doing here?"

"Waitin'. After yer ma died, seemed like I didn't care t' work fer no other privit fam'ly, so I came back here on my old job. I'll bet I'm the homeliest head-waitress in captivity."

Ted's nervous fingers were pleating the tablecloth. His voice sank to a whisper. "Birdie, tell me the God's truth. Did those three years cause her death?"

"Niver!" lied Birdie. "I was with her to the end. It started with a cold on th' chest. Have some French fried with yer beef, Mr. Teddy. They're illigant today."

Birdie glided off to the kitchen. Authors are fond of the word "glide." But you can take it literally this time. Birdie had a face that looked like a huge mistake, but she walked like a panther, and they're said to be the last cry as gliders. She walked with her chin up and her hips firm. That comes from juggling trays. You have to walk like that to keep your nose out of the soup. After a while the walk becomes a habit. Any seasoned dining-room girl could give lessons in walking to the Delsarte teacher of an Eastern finishing school.

From the day that Birdie Callahan served Ted with the roast beef medium and the elegant French fried, she appointed herself monitor over his food and clothes and morals. I wish I could find words to describe his bitter loneliness. He did not seek companionship. The men, although not directly avoiding him, seemed somehow to have pressing business whenever they happened in his vicinity. The women ignored him. Mrs. Dankworth, still dashing and still widowed, passed Ted one day and looked fixedly at a point one inch above his head. In a town like ours the Haley House is like a big, hospitable clubhouse. The men drop in there the first thing in the morning, and the last thing at night, to hear the gossip and buy a cigar and jolly the girl at the cigar counter. Ted spoke to them when they spoke to him. He began to develop a certain grim line about the mouth. Joe Haley watched him from afar, and the longer he watched the kinder and more speculative grew the look in his eyes. And slowly and surely there grew in the hearts of our townspeople a certain new respect and admiration for this boy who was fighting his fight.

Ted got into the habit of taking his meals late, so that Birdie Callahan could take the time to talk to him.

"Birdie," he said one day, when she brought his soup, "do you know that you're the only decent woman who'll talk to me? Do you know what I mean when I say that I'd give the rest of my life if I could just put my head in my mother's lap and have her muss up my hair and call me foolish names?" Birdie Callahan cleared her throat and said abruptly: "I was noticin' yesterday your gray pants need pressin' bad. Bring 'em down tomorrow mornin' and I'll give 'em th' elegant crease in the laundry."

So the first weeks went by, and the two months of Miss Wenzel's stay came to an end. Ted thanked his God and tried hard not to wish that she was a man so that he could punch her head.

The day before the time appointed for her departure she was closeted with Joe Haley for a long, long time. When finally she emerged a bellboy lounged up to Ted with a message. "Wenzel says th' Old Man wants t' see you. 'S in his office. Say, Mr. Terrill, do yuh think they can play today? It's pretty wet."

Joe Haley was sunk in the depths of his big leather chair. He did not look up as Ted entered. "Sit down," he said. Ted sat down and waited, puzzled.

"As a wizard at figures," mused Joe Haley at last, softly as though to himself, "I'm a frost. A column of figures on paper makes my head swim. But I can carry a whole regiment of 'em in my head. I know every time the barkeeper draws one in the dark. I've been watchin' this thing for the last two weeks hopin' you'd quit and come and tell me." He turned suddenly and faced Ted. "Ted, old kid," he said sadly, "what'n'ell made you do it again?"

"What's the joke?" asked Ted.

"Now, Ted," remonstrated Joe Haley, "that way of talkin' won't help matters none. As I said, I'm rotten at figures. But you're the first investment that ever turned out bad, and let me tell you I've handled some mighty bad-smelling ones. Why, kid, if you had just come to me on the quiet and asked for the loan of a hundred or so, why—"

"What's the joke, Joe?" said Ted again, slowly.

"This ain't my notion of a joke," came the terse answer. "We're $300 short."

The last vestige of Ted Terrill's old-time radiance seemed to flicker and die, leaving him ashen and old.

"Short?" he repeated. Then, "My God!" in a strangely colorless voice—"My God!" He looked down at his fingers impersonally, as though they belonged to someone else. Then his hand clutched Joe Haley's arm with the grip of fear. "Joe! Joe! That's the thing that has haunted me day and night, till my nerves are raw. The fear of doing it again. Don't laugh at me, will you? I used to lie awake nights going over that cursed business of the bank—over and over—till the cold sweat would break out all over me. I used to figure it all out again, step by step, until—Joe, could a man steal and not know it? Could thinking of a thing like that drive a man crazy? Because if it could—if it could—then—"

"I don't know," said Joe Haley, "but it sounds darned fishy." He had a hand on Ted's shaking shoulder, and was looking into the white, drawn face. "I had great plans for you, Ted. But Minnie Wenzel's got it all down on slips of paper. I might as well call her in again, and we'll have the whole blamed thing out."

Minnie Wenzel came. In her hand were slips of paper, and books with figures in them, and Ted looked and saw things written in his own hand that should not have been there. And he covered his shamed face with his two hands and gave thanks that his mother was dead.

There came three sharp raps at the office door. The tense figures within jumped nervously.

"Keep out!" called Joe Haley, "whoever you are." Whereupon the door opened and Birdie Callahan breezed in.

"Get out, Birdie Callahan," roared Joe. "You're in the wrong pew."

Birdie closed the door behind her composedly and came farther into the room. "Pete th' pasthry cook just tells me that Minnie Wenzel told th' day clerk, who told the barkeep, who told th' janitor, who told th' chef, who told Pete, that Minnie had caught Ted stealin' some $300."

Ted took a quick step forward. "Birdie, for Heaven's sake, keep out of this. You can't make things any better. You may believe in me, but—"

"Where's the money?" asked Birdie. Ted stared at her a moment, his mouth open ludicrously.

"Why—I—don't—know," articulated, painfully. "I never thought of that."

Birdie snorted defiantly. "I thought so. D'ye know," sociably, "I was visitin' with my aunt Mis' Mulcahy last evenin'."

There was a quick rustle of silks from Minnie Wenzel's direction.

"Say, look here—" began Joe Haley, impatiently.

"Shut up, Joe Haley!" snapped Birdie. "As I was sayin', I was visitin' with my aunt Mis' Mulcahy. She does fancy washin' an' ironin' for the swells. An' Minnie Wenzel, there bein' none sweller, hires her to do up her weddin' linens. Such smears av hand embridery an' Irish crochet she never see th' likes, Mis' Mulcahy says, and she's seen a lot. And as a special treat to the poor owld soul, why Minnie Wenzel lets her see some av her weddin' clothes. There never yet was a woman who cud resist showin' her weddin' things to every other woman she cud lay hands on. Well, Mis' Mulcahy, she see that grand trewsow and she said she never saw th' beat. Dresses! Well, her going-away suit alone comes to $80, for it's bein' made by Molkowsky, the little Polish tailor. An' her weddin dress is satin, do yuh mind! Oh, it was a real treat for my aunt Mis' Mulcahy."

Birdie walked over to where Minnie Wenzel sat, very white and still, and pointed a stubby red finger in her face. " 'Tis the grand manager ye are, Miss Wenzel, gettin' satins an' tailor-mades on yer salary. It takes a woman, Minnie Wenzel, to see through a woman's thricks."

"Well I'll be dinged!" exploded Joe Haley.

"Yuh'd better be!" retorted Birdie Callahan.

Minnie Wenzel stood up, her lip caught between her teeth.

"Am I to understand, Joe Haley, that you dare to accuse me of taking your filthy money, instead of that miserable ex-con there who has done time?"

"That'll do, Minnie," said Joe Haley, gently. "That's a-plenty."

"Prove it," went on Minnie, and then looked as though she wished she hadn't.

"A business college edjication is a grand foine thing," observed Birdie, "Miss Wenzel is a graduate av wan. They teach you everything from drawin' birds with tail feathers to plain and fancy penmanship. In fact, they teach everything in the writin' line except forgery, an' I ain't so sure they haven't got a coorse in that."

"I don't care," whimpered Minnie Wenzel suddenly, sinking in a limp heap on the floor. "I had to do it. I'm marrying a swell fellow and a girl's got to have some clothes that don't look like a Bird Center dressmaker's work. He's got three sisters. I saw their pictures and they're coming to the wedding. They're the kind that wear low-necked dresses in the evening, and have their hair and nails done downtown. I haven't got a thing but looks. Could I go to New York dressed like a rube? On the square, Joe, I worked here six years and never took a sou. But things got away from me. The tailor wouldn't finish my suit unless I paid him $50 down. I only took 50 at first, intending to pay it back. Honest to goodness, Joe, I did."

"Cut it out," said Joe Haley, "and get up. I was going to give you a check for your wedding, though I hadn't counted on no 300. We'll call it square. And I hope you'll be happy, but I don't gamble on it. You'll be goin' through your man's pants before you're married a year. You can take your hat and fade. I'd like to know how I'm ever going to square this thing with Ted and Birdie."

"An' me standin' gassin' while them fool girls in the dinin'-room can't set a table decent, and dinner in less than ten minutes," cried Birdie, rushing off. Ted mumbled something unintelligible and at once was after her.

"Birdie! I want to talk to you," he said earnestly.

"Say it quick then," said Birdie, over her shoulder. "The doors open in three minnits."

"I can't tell you how grateful I am. This is no place to talk to you. Will you let me walk home with you tonight after your work's done?"

"Will I?" said Birdie, turning to face him. "I will not. Th' swell mob has shook you, an' a good thing it is. You was travelin' with a bunch of racers, when you was only built for medium speed. Now you've got your chance to a fresh start and don't you ever think I'm going to be the one to let you spoil it by beginnin' to walk out with a dinin'-room Lizzie like me."

"Don't say that, Birdie," Ted put in.

"It's the truth," affirmed Birdie. "Not that I ain't a perfec'ly respectable girrul, and ye know it. I'm a good slob, but folks would be tickled for the chance to say that you had nobody to go with but the likes av me. If I was to let you walk home with me tonight, yuh might be askin' to call next week. Inside half a year, if yuh was lonesome enough, yuh'd ask me to marry yuh. And b'gorra," she said softly, looking down at her unlovely red hands, "I'm dead scared I'd do it. Get back to work, Ted Terrill, and hold yer head up high, and when yuh say your prayers tonight, thank your lucky stars I ain't a hussy."

Rien Ne Va Plus

by **Alexander Woollcott**

WE WERE SITTING UNDER the midsummer stars at Monte Carlo eating a soufflé and talking about suicide, when a passing newsmonger stopped at our table all aglow with the tidings that that young American with the white forelock had just been found crumpled on the beach, a bullet-hole in his heart. Earlier in the evening—it was shortly before we came out of the Casino in quest of dinner—we had all seen him wiped out by a final disastrous turn of the wheel. And now he lay dead on the shore.

I shall have to admit that the news gave a fillip to the occasion. It came towards the end of a long, luscious dinner on the terrace opposite the Casino. We were a casually assembled carful, who had driven over from

Antibes in the late afternoon, planning to play a little roulette as an appetizer and then to dine interminably.

When we had arrived in the *Salles Privées* a few hours before, there was only standing room around our table at first. In this rapt fringe I encountered Sam Fletcher, a dawdling journalist who lived on occasional assignments from the Paris offices of American newspapers. He pointed out the notables to me. There was Mary Garden, for instance, playing intently, losing and winning, losing and winning, with that economy of emotional expenditure which one usually reserves for setting-up exercises. Then there was an English dowager who looked as though she were held together by adhesive type. She was betting parsimoniously, but Fletcher whispered to me that she lived in Monte Carlo on an ample allowance provided by her son-in-law, with the sole stipulation that she never embarrass the family by coming home. A moribund remittance woman. Next to her sat a pallid old gentleman whose hands, as they caressed his stack of counters, were conspicuously encased in braided gloves of gray silk. It seems that in his youth he had been a wastrel, and on her deathbed his mother had squeezed from him a solemn promise never to touch card or chip again as long as he lived.

As for young White Lock, there was, until his final bet, nothing else noticeable about him except that he was the only man then at the table wearing a dinner coat. We heard later that at first he had lost heavily and had had to make several trips to the *caisse* to replenish his supply of plaques. By the time I came along he had settled to a more cautious play but finally, as if from boredom, he took all his plaques and counters and stacked them on the red. To this pile he added, just as the wheel began to turn, the contents of his wallet—emptying out a small cascade of thousand-franc notes, with a single hundred-franc note among them. But this one he retrieved at the last moment as if to be sure of carfare home. There was that breathless spinning movement, then the fateful *"Rien ne va plus,"* issuing in the same dead voice with which the intoning of the mass falls on infidel ears. Then the decision, *"Noir."* Around that table you could hear the word for black being *exhaled* in every language the world has known since Babel.

The young man gave a little laugh as the *croupier* called the turn. He sat quite still as his last gauge was raked into the bank. With all eyes on him, he shoved his chair back from the table, reached for his wallet, took out the aforesaid hundred-franc note and pushed it, with white, fastidious fingers, toward the center of the patterned baize. *"Pour le personnel,"* he said, with a kind of wry grandeur which hushed the usual twitter of thanks from the *croupiers.* "And that," he added, "is that." So saying, he got to his feet, yawned a little, and sauntered out of the room. I remember thinking, at the time, that he was behaving rather like any desperate young man in any Zoë Akins play. But it was a good performance. And now, it seemed, he lay dead by the water's edge.

It was Fletcher himself who brought the news. It came, I say, just as we were eating soufflé and talking of suicide. This, of course, was no obliging coincidence. One always tells tales of self-slaughter at Monte Carlo. It is part of the legend of the principality—as strong in its force of suggestion, I suppose, as the legend of Lourdes is strong in its hint to hysterics that the time has come to cast away their crutches. Fletcher told us that the sound of the shot had brought a watchman running. The youth lay on his back, his chin tilted to the stars, one outstretched hand limply holding the revolver, a dark stain on the pleated whiteness of his breast. Before Fletcher could wire his report to Paris, he would have to await certain—well—formalities. In a conspiratorial whisper, he explained there had been so many such suicides of late that a new rule was but recently put into effect. Whenever any client of the Casino was found self-slain with empty pockets, it was customary for the Casino to rush a bankroll to the spot before notifying the police, so that the victim would seem to have ended it all from *Weltschmerz.* Even now, Fletcher said, this trick must be in progress, and in the meantime he ought to be seeking such obituary data as might be gleaned in the registry office.

We were still lingering over our coffee when he came hurrying back to us, all bristling with the end of the story.

Notified in due course, the *gendarmerie* had repaired to the beach in quest of the body. But there was none. Not at the indicated spot, nor anywhere else on the shore. After further search, the minor chieftain from the Casino, who had himself tucked 10,000 francs into the pocket of the now missing suicide and was still lurking, much puzzled, in the middle-distance, returned at last to the *Salles Privées,* only to find them humming with a new chapter. It seems that that young American with the white forelock—the one somebody or other had inaccurately reported as killed—had reappeared, apparently restored in spirits, and certainly restored in funds. He had bet tremendously, lingered for only three turns of the wheel, and departed with 100,000 francs. The attendants assumed he had merely been out to dinner. At least, the careless fellow had spilled some tomato sauce on his shirt front.

Four-and-Twenty Blackjacks

by **S. J. Perelman**

THE MINUTES OF THE OXFORD UNION for 1920—a copy of which is, of course, readily available at everyone's elbow—reveal that during its entire winter session that world-famed discussion group and conventicle of pundits was sunk in a mood of almost suicidal despair. The honourable members, thitherto scornful of American eloquence, had become so alarmed at the rhetoric stemming from the Classical High School Debating Society in Providence, Rhode Island, that they were seriously considering mass hara-kiri. "What is the sense of we tongue-tied slobs beating our gums," lamented one Balliol man, summing up the universal sentiment, "when these brilliant Yank speechifiers in faraway New England, every man jack of them a Cicero or Demosthenes, has made a chump out of us oratorywise?" His defeatism was well grounded; week after week, in a series of dazzling intramural debates, the Rhode Island striplings were exhibiting a fluency rivalling that of Edmund Burke and the elder Pitt on such varied topics as "Resolved: That the Philippines Be Given Their Independence," "Resolved: That the End Justifies the Means," and "Resolved: That the Pen Is Mightier Than the Sword." It was a great natural phenomenon, as inexplicable as parthenogenesis or the strapless bra, and I still feel cocky that I should have presided over it as chairman of the society—well, chairman pro tem, which is almost the same thing. The descendants of Roger Williams don't go in for lousy little distinctions.

The club met every Wednesday afternoon in a classroom that generations of adolescent males had endowed with the reek of a pony stable. It shied a few erasers about to insure a proper concentration of chalk dust in the lungs, and then, as an aperitif to the polemics, listened to an original paper read by one of the membership. Most of these treatises were on fairly cosmic themes; I myself contributed a philippic entitled "Science vs. Religion," an indigestible hash of Robert Ingersoll and Haldeman-Julius, in which I excoriated the Vatican and charged it, under pain of my displeasure, to mend its ways before our next meeting. Occasionally, somebody would alter the pattern and deliver an essay in lighter vein, on, say, "The Witchery of Jack Frost" or "Squeteague Fishing."

Though parliamentary procedure was mother's milk to me, and it was self-evident that I was marked out for political leadership, an altogether fortuitous circumstance scotched my career. One afternoon, while refereeing a tedious forensic battle on the single tax, I somehow lost the thread and became absorbed in a book about a gentleman cracksman called "The Adventures of Jimmie Dale," by Frank L. Packard. To this day, I cannot account for my psychological brownout; I assume it sprang from the heavy burden of administrative anxieties I was carrying. At any rate, enthralled with the melodrama, I did not discover that the meeting had adjourned until I found Mr. Bludyer, the principal, shaking me violently. He told me that various restoratives, among them my own gavel, had been tried on me without effect and that finally I had been cashiered. "I'd take up some pastime that doesn't tax the intellect, like volleyball," he suggested pointedly. That I went on to score notable gridiron successes and overnight become the idol of the school is unimportant. It was only when the B. M. C. Durfee High School, of Fall River, kayoed us on the issue "Resolved: That Cigarette Smoking Is Injurious to Our Youth" that my rueful colleagues realized the price they had paid for their inconstancy.

Quite recently, at Kaliski & Gabay's auction parlors, I was whipsawed into buying Packard's fable as part of a job lot of second-hand books, and, faced with the dilemma of rereading it or being certified as a spendthrift incapable of handling his own funds, I chose the coward's way. Before I could get into the story, though, I was sidetracked by the publisher's advertisement in the flyleaves, a sample of the quaint propaganda used in 1917 to popularize the habit of reading. There was nothing like reading, affirmed the A. L. Burt Company, "for a hardworking man, after his daily toil, or in its intervals. It calls for no bodily exertion." The statement may have been true of the four hundred titles that followed, but not of "The Adventures of Jimmie Dale." Its previous owner had apparently read it while sipping mucilage, for whole episodes were gummed together in the most repulsive fashion. Between prying them apart with a fruit knife, geeing up the fragments, and retrieving the book from the wastebasket, into which it unaccountably kept sliding like a greased pig, I was almost as pooped as the time I whitewashed a three-room henhouse singlehanded.

To anyone who has ever worked his way out of a

boxwood maze, the plot of Packard's novel offers no problem, but a supply of pine-knot torches, pickaxes, and shredded paper are indispensable kit for the tyro reader. Each of the two central characters, for example—Jimmie Dale and Marie LaSalle—has three distinct identities. Jimmie is a young millionaire bachelor, an elusive safecracker known as the Gray Seal, and a derelict hophead called Larry the Bat; Marie, likewise rich and socially elite (though forced into hiding by malefactors who crave her money), poses sometimes as the Tocsin, a shadowy fingerwoman, and again as Silver Mag, a disreputable old crone. The lives of the pair—or, more precisely, the six—are forever being sought by scores of hoodlums, gunsels, informers, shyster lawyers, and crooked shamuses, so that they are constantly compelled to switch roles. The upshot is that you are never very positive who is assaulting whom; once or twice, I got the panicky impression that Jimmie's alter egos were throttling each other. This imaginative twist, somewhat akin to the old vaudeville specialty of Desiretta, the Man Who Wrestles with Himself, proved erroneous when I checked up. It was just a couple of other felons.

Obeying the basic canon that romances about gentleman cracksmen begin in ultra-exclusive clubs, "The Adventures of Jimmie Dale" begins in one called the St. James and omits no traditional touch. Herman Carruthers, crusading young editor of the *News-Argus,* is dealing out the usual expository flapdoodle about the Gray Seal ("the kingpin of them all, the most puzzling, bewildering, delightful crook in the annals of crime") to Jimmie, who is so bland, quizzical, and mocking that even the busboys must be aware he is the marauder himself. His blandness grows practically intolerable when Carruthers avers that the kingpin is dead, for, as he and any five-year-old criminologist know, the kingpin is merely dormant until society needs his philanthropic assist. The summons reaches Jimmie that very midnight, at his luxurious Riverside Drive mansion, in the form of a note from the mysterious feminine mastermind he has never seen, who directs all his exploits. With a curious, cryptic smile tingeing his lips, Jimmie opens his safe and removes exactly what you would expect: "It was not an ordinary belt; it was full of stout-sewn, upright little pockets all the way around, and in the pockets grimly lay an array of fine, blued-steel, highly tempered instruments—a compact, powerful burglar's kit." Half an hour later, an inconspicuous figure flits downtown via Washington Square. Except for the black silk mask, the slouch hat pulled well down over his eyes, and the automatic revolver and electric flashlight, nobody would ever suspect him of being a Raffles.

The actual caper Jimmie executes is too intricate and

inconsequential to warrant recapitulating; briefly, by leaving his telltale Gray Seal on a rifled safe, he saves from prison a character who, in behalf of his ailing wife, has heisted his employer's funds. A civic uproar ensues: "The Morning *News-Argus* offered twenty-five thousand dollars reward for the capture of the Gray Seal! Other papers immediately followed suit in varying amounts. The authorities, State and municipal, goaded to desperation, did likewise, and the five million men, women, and children of New York were automatically metamorphosed into embryonic sleuths. New York was aroused." It seems odd that such a *brouhaha* should attend a misdemeanor approximately as monstrous as spitting in the subway, but, no doubt, Manhattan was more strait-laced in that epoch. On the heels of the foregoing comes another sensation—the body of a stool pigeon with alleged evidence linking his murder to the Gray Seal. Our hero's every sensibility is outraged: "Anger, merciless and unrestrained, surged over Jimmie Dale. . . . Even worse to Jimmie Dale's artistic and sensitive temperament was the vilification, the holding up to loathing, contumely, and abhorrence of the name, the stainless name, of the Gray Seal. It *was* stainless! He had guarded it jealously—as a man guards the woman's name he loves." Eyes flashing like cut-steel buckles, he retires to the slum hideout he calls the Sanctuary and revamps himself into Larry the Bat: "His fingers worked quickly—a little wax behind the ears, in the nostrils, under the upper lip, deftly placed—hands, wrists, neck, throat, and face received their quota of stain, applied with an artist's touch—and then the spruce, muscular Jimmie Dale, transformed into a slouching, vicious-featured denizen of the underworld, replaced the box under the flooring, pulled a slouch hat over his eyes, extinguished the gas, and went out." By dint of certain devious researches, which I could not extricate from the glue, a venal police inspector is unmasked as the culprit and the Gray Seal absolved. If my calculations are correct, Jimmie in the first sixty pages of the action has enjoyed a grand total of eleven minutes sleep, considerably less than the most wide-awake reader.

Stimulated to a healthy glow by these finger exercises, Jimmie now dashes off an ambitious four-part fugue plangent with larceny and homicide. Under the pretense of glomming a diamond chaplet from the strongbox of a rascally broker, he recovers a note held by the Scrooge against a mining engineer he has fleeced, bilks a ring of counterfeiters blackmailing a sheep in their toils, robs a dealer of gems to obviate his being slaughtered by yeggs (a curious bit of preventive surgery), and exposes a knavish banker named Carling who has looted his own vaults and pinned the blame on an underling with a criminal record. In the last-named coup, the accused has a winsome infant, enabling Packard to pull out the *vox-humana* stop when Jimmie extorts the vital confession: " 'Carling,' said Jimmie hoarsely, 'I stood beside a little bed tonight and looked at a baby girl—a little baby girl with golden hair, who smiled as she slept. . . . Take this pen, or—this.' The automatic lifted until the muzzle was on a line with Carling's eyes." Jimmie's antisocial behavior, it goes without saying, never redounds to his personal advantage; he scrupulously returns all swag to its rightful owners and, even while bashing in whatever skulls deserve it, exudes the high moral purpose of his progenitor Robin Hood. True, he betrays a pallid romantic interest in the Maid Marian who animates him from behind the scenes, but nothing that would boil an egg. In the light of contemporary pulp fiction, one marvels that Packard spiced his famous goulash with so little sexual paprika. Perhaps it may be possible to sublimate the libido by twiddling the combination of a Herring-Hall-Marvin safe, or, on the other hand, perhaps the kid's just a medical curiosity. Nobody could be *that* dedicated.

And yet he is, unless you discount the evidence of the next hundred pages. In rapid succession, he clears the reputation of a putative ruby thief, brings to book the architect of a payroll killing and his henchmen, and restores the stolen map of a gold mine to the widow and children of its legal claimant. There is a magnificent consistency about Packard's minor figures; other writers may muck about with halftones and nuances, but his widows are all destitute and enfeebled and his villains are rotten to the core. A typical sample is the satanic attorney who conceived the payroll incident above: "Gunning, shrewd, crafty, conscienceless, cold-blooded—that was Stangeist . . . the six-foot muscular frame, that was invariably clothed in attire of the most fashionable cut; the thin lips with their oily, plausible smile, the straight black hair that straggled into pin-point, little black eyes, the dark face with its high cheekbones, which, with the pronounced aquiline nose and the persistent rumor that he was a quarter caste, had led the underworld, prejudiced always in favor of a 'monaker,' to dub the man the 'Indian Chief.' " A Choctaw version of Louis Calhern in "The Asphalt Jungle," you might say, and a real ripsnorter. The argot in which the crooks converse also has the same classical purity; *vide* that of the Weasel, an obscure cutpurse who stirs recollections of Happy Hooligan, of sainted memory; "Why, youse damned fool," jeered the Weasel, "d'youse t'ink youse can get away wid dat? Say, take it from me, youse are a piker! Say, youse make me tired. Wot d'youse t'ink youse are? D'youse t'ink dis is a tee-ayter, an' dat youse are a cheap-skate actor strollin' acrost the stage?" Scant wonder, with such nostalgic Chimmie Fadden dialogue, that youse has to swallow repeatedly to exorcise de lump in de t'roat.

The machine-gun tempo, to use a flabby designation, slackens momentarily for an interview in the dark between Jimmie and the Tocsin, his female control. His work is nearing completion, she whispers, and soon she can disclose herself with impunity. This, as the intuitive will guess, is the conventional literary strip tease, because in the next breath the deluge descends. The Crime Club—not the Doubleday fellows, but "the most powerful and pitiless organization of criminals the world has ever known"—pounces on the dapper thief. In a scary milieu replete with hydraulic walls, sliding laboratories, and a binful of putty noses and false whiskers, its minions vainly ply him with a truth drug to elicit word of the Tocsin's whereabouts. No contusions result, except to the laws of English syntax, and Jimmie is let out to pasture. It would only court neuralgia to retrace the labyrinthine steps by which the author maneuvers him into the arms of his lady, now disguised as Silver Mag, the beggarwoman, but ultimately the lovebirds make contact and the lava spills over: "The warm, rich lips were yielding to his; he could feel that throb, the life in the young, lithe form against his own. She was his—his! The years, the past, all were swept away—and she was his at last—his for always. And there came a mighty sense of kingship upon him, as though all the world were at his feet, and virility, and a great, glad strength above all other men's, and a song was in his soul, a song triumphant—for she was his!" In other words, she was his, *Gott sei dank,* and you have just burst into sobs of relief when the whole confounded business begins over again. Marie LaSalle, alias the Tocsin, alias Silver Mag, pours out a long, garbled *histoire,* the kernel of which is that the head of the Crime Club, posing as her uncle, seeks to kill her for her estate. Jimmie manages to worm a confession from him clinching his guilt; in the attendant melee, though, he is recognized as the Gray Seal, and a wrathful mob of vigilantes from the Tenderloin tracks him to the Sanctuary and puts it to the torch. The lovers providentially escape over the rooftops to continue their didos in "The Further Adventures of Jimmie Dale," "Jimmie Dale and the Phantom Clue," and "Jimmie Dale and the Blue Envelope," and blessed silence descends, broken only by the scratch of Packard's pen endorsing his royalty checks.

I was in a Sixth Avenue bus, traffic-bound in Herald Square, when I finished the last three chapters, and a natural impulse to break clean made me drop the book into the vacant seat before me. Moments later, a brace of speedy sixteen-year-olds in windbreakers emblazoned with side elevations of Jane Russell crash-dived into the seat and buried themselves in comics. One of them suddenly detected the volume nestling against his spine. "Hey!" he exclaimed. "Someone lost a book." "It ain't a book. There's no pictures in it," his companion corrected. Together they laboriously spelled out the title and joined in a quick, incurious survey of the contents. "Ah, just a lot of slush," observed the first, in disdain. "What kind of an old creep'd get a charge out of this stuff?" An old creep directly behind them turned blush-pink, fastened his eyes on a Mojud stocking and strove to retain his dignity. At Forty-second Street, weary of their tiresome speculation and guffaws, he disembarked, not, however, without a shrivelling glance. If you ask me, popinjays like that, and all these young whippersnappers you meet nowadays, have no more character than a tin pie plate. Why, at their age I was already chairman of a world-famed debating society.

Stop Me—If You've Heard This One

by **Ring Lardner**

On a certain day in the year 1927, Jerry Blades and Luke Garner, young playwrights, entered the Lambs' Club at the luncheon hour and were beckoned to a corner table by an actor friend, Charley Speed. Charley had a guest, recognized at once by the newcomers as Henry Wild Osborne, famous globe-trotter, raconteur, and banquet-hall fixture.

"Sit down, boys," said Charley after he had introduced them to the celebrity. "I'm due at a house committee meeting and you can keep Harry entertained."

But "Harry" proved perfectly capable of providing his own entertainment and theirs, and he opened up with a barrage of Pats and Mikes, Ikeys and Jakeys, and MacPhersons and MacDonalds that were not only comparatively new but also quite funny—at least, so Blades and Garner judged from the whole-hearted laughter of the narrator himself.

When he had displayed his mastery of all the different dialects of both hemispheres, he related a few personal adventures, in some of which other big men had played parts and which, to his small audience, were much more interesting than the chronicles concerning fictional Mikes, Sandys, and Abes. He told them of Lindbergh, who had accepted an invitation to dine with him in his apartment and had come wearing a hat that did not fit, explaining he had borrowed it at his hotel, not having had a hat of his own since he was a child.

"He's a man of one idea. He will talk about aviation and nothing else. He dislikes crowds and has had difficulty maintaining a show of good nature in the face of unwelcome attention. He has managed to do so, however, excepting when addressed or referred to as 'Lucky Lindy,' a nickname he just can't stand.

"He was kind enough to ask me to fly with him on Long Island and naturally I jumped at the chance. We took a taxi out to the field and every traffic cop on the way stopped us so they could shake hands with him and pat him on the back. I thought we'd never get there, and when we did get there, that we wouldn't be able to leave the ground without killing two or three hundred people.

"He said it was like that every time he attempted to go up or land—hundreds of wild-eyed fans crowding around him in spite of the danger. But we did finally get started and it was wonderful. I felt as safe as if I'd been riding in a chair at Atlantic City."

He told them of Fred Stone—of an occasion when he and Fred had dined together at old Rector's. At the next table were two famous Princeton football players, each over six feet tall and weighing two hundred and twenty pounds. The sons of Old Nassau had been drinking something contentious and tried to pick a quarrel with him and Stone, though they had no idea who Stone and Osborne were and certainly could have had no reason to "fuss" at either of them.

Fred did not want to make a scene and ignored the athletes' slurring remarks, but when he and Osborne got up to leave and the Princeton boys followed and jostled them, the comedian lost his temper, grasped a collegiate throat in each hand, lifted the pair up bodily, and knocked their heads together till they were unconscious, and then tossed them into the checkroom.

He told them of having been in the Metropole at supper with Herman Rosenthal the night the gambler was called away from the table and shot to death by four gangsters; of having warned Jim Jeffries not to drink the tea that "poisoned" him just prior to the fight with Jack Johnson; of having tipped off Kid Gleason in 1919 that some of his ballplayers were throwing him down; of having accompanied General Pershing to Marshal Foch's headquarters when the American commander offered his armies to the Frenchman to do with as he pleased; of having escaped death by eight inches when the Germans dropped their first bombs on Paris; of having taught Lloyd Waner how to avoid always hitting to left field, of having taken Irving Berlin out of "Mike's" place and set him to writing songs; of having advised Flo Ziegfeld to dress his chorus in skirts instead of tights; of having suggested and helped organize the Actors' Equity; and of having informed the Indiana police where to find Gerald Chapman.

He had been everywhere and seen everything, and Blades and Garner envied him his wealth of experience.

He hoped he hadn't bored them.

"Not at all!" said Blades.

"It's a treat to listen to you," said Garner.

"You ought to write a book of memoirs," said Blades.

"I've been urged to many times," said Osborne, "but I'm never in one place long enough to get at it. I've got chronic wanderlust."

"So have I," said Garner, "but it doesn't do me any good."

"Poor Luke!" said Blades. "He'd like to live on trains, but he's only been out of the state once."

"Not counting two or three trips to Newark," said Garner.

"Travel is a great thing!" observed Osborne. "It has its drawbacks and discomforts, but one's experiences and adventures are worth a lot more than they cost."

"Luke had a queer little experience the only time he went anywhere," said Blades. "Tell Mr. Osborne about it, Luke."

"Oh, it's nothing much. Just a kind of mystery I was mixed up in on the way out to Chicago."

"Let's hear it," said Osborne.

"Well," said young Garner, "I'll try to make it brief. About a year ago I had an idea for a play. I wrote one act and read it to George M. Cohan. He liked it and told me to finish it and bring it to him. When I had finished it, I learned he was in Chicago. I couldn't wait for him to get back, so I decided to go out there and see him, though I had to borrow money for the trip. I was impatient and took the Twentieth Century.

"In the section across from me there was one of the most beautiful women I ever saw—a young woman about twenty-five, dark, well dressed, full of class, nice-looking. She had a book, one of J. S. Fletcher's detective stories, but I noticed she didn't turn more than three pages between New York and Albany. Most of the time she just stared at the river.

"She was going to Chicago, too, and I'll confess that I wished we would become acquainted long before we got there. I wished it, but didn't believe it, because she was evidently not the kind you could meet unconventionally.

"I went in the diner about seven and was given the only vacant chair at a table for four. My table companions were an elderly couple and a man a little older than I, a man of striking appearance, handsome, and dark enough to suggest Spanish or Italian ancestry.

"The elderly couple finished their meal and left. The 'Spaniard' was just beginning to eat when the girl from my car came in and took one of the seats just vacated.

"Her glance and the 'Spaniard's' met. There was mutual recognition and an emotion close to panic on both sides. The man got up hurriedly, put a five-dollar bill on the table, and went out of the diner, toward the front end of the train. The girl grasped the table as if she must have something to hang on to. She was utterly white and I thought she was going to faint. She didn't, but her hands shook violently as she wrote her order.

"I pretended I had not observed the little scene and did my best not to look in her direction. I got through as quickly as I could and relieved her of the embarrassment of my presence. As I was paying my check, the waiter asked me if I knew whether the other man was coming back. Before I could reply, the girl said, 'No,' then bit her lip as if she were mad at herself for speaking.

"She returned to her section after a long time, over an hour. She sat staring out into the darkness for a half hour more. Then she got up and stepped across the aisle to me and said, 'I must ask you to do me a favor. You will think it's queer, but I can't help it. You saw the man leave the table when I sat down. I want you to find him and give him this note. I would ask the porter, but I am afraid he might give it to the wrong person. The man is probably in the club car. Just hand him the note. Then come back and tell me. Will you do it?'

"I found him in the club car, delivered the note she had intrusted to me, and returned and reported.

"She said, 'I am very, very grateful.'

"And then I went forward to the club car again and sat down to be out of the way when he came to her, as I felt sure he would.

"He was at the desk writing, but soon he rose and left. I was in quite a fever of curiosity and it strained my will power to stay where I was and not follow him and witness 'Act Two.' I tried to read and couldn't. When I finally turned in, close to midnight, the girl's berth was dark and the curtains drawn.

"I got up at Elkhart. The curtains were open across the aisle, but there was no sign of the girl. There was still no sign of her as we pulled into Englewood. I called the porter and asked whether he had seen her since the night before. He said why, yes, he had seen her around five o'clock, when he had helped her off the train at Toledo. 'Toledo!' I exclaimed. 'I thought she was going through.' The porter said he had thought so, too, but she must have changed her mind. I inquired if he had seen her talking with a handsome dark man. He said no; that the only real dark man he had seen on that car was himself, and he wasn't handsome.

"I stood on the platform in the La Salle Street Station till all the passengers were off. The girl was not among them; I'm sure of that. But the 'Spaniard' was, and escorting him were two men who were obviously detectives.

"In the two days I was there, I read every story in every paper, trying to find a solution to 'my mystery,' but without success. And that's all there is to it, except that Mr. Cohan turned down my play."

"Very interesting!" Mr. Osburne remarked. "I believe if I had been you, I'd have followed the man and his escort, just to satisfy my curiosity."

"I'd have done that," said Garner, "if I hadn't thought there was still a chance that the girl would appear."

Charley Speed was back from the committee meeting. He and his guest bade the young playwrights goodbye and went out. Blades and Garner discussed the man they had just met.

"He tells dialect stories well," said Blades.

"If that's possible," said Garner. "To me, his own experiences are a lot more interesting."

"But I think," said Blades slowly, "I think somebody else told me that same stuff about Lindbergh and—"

"Yes," interrupted Garner, "and I'm under the impression that the one about Fred Stone isn't new to me. In fact, I'm pretty sure I heard it from Rex Beach and that Rex was with Stone when it happened."

Two years later Blades and Garner, now credited with a couple of Broadway hits, were guests at a "small" dinner party given by Wallace Gore, the publisher. Their host presented them to Mr. Henry Wild Osborne, who acknowledged the introduction as if it were a novelty.

Osborne sat between two adoring women who managed to keep him to themselves through the soup. But he was everybody's property and soon was regaling the whole table with up-to-the-minute episodes in the careers of Pat, Abe, and MacPherson. He ran out of them at last and his host said, "Harry, I wonder if you'd mind telling these people about your Chicago trip."

"What Chicago trip?"

"About the girl and the foreigner."

"Oh, that!" said Osborne. "Well, if you think they'd be interested."

"Of course they would!"

"Please, Mr. Osborne!"

"All right, then," said Osborne, "but I trust you folks not to spread it around. The Chicago police made a secret of the real facts and I promised them I wouldn't divulge it to any of my friends of the Fourth Estate."

He took a swallow of wine and began: "It was a month ago I had a wire from Charlie Dawes, asking me to come out there and advise him in a little matter—well, we won't go into that. I boarded the Broadway Limited and was settling down to a little session with de Maupassant when I noticed a beautiful girl, an authentic, perfect blonde, in the section across from me.

"I am past the age of train flirtations but this girl held my attention by the expression on her face, a look of ineffable sadness, of tragic longing for—I knew not what.

"I was weaving in my mind a blighted romance with her as its sorrowing heroine when Andy Mellon, walking through the car, saw me and stopped for a chat.

He was with me till dinner-time, when he invited me to dine in his drawing-room, but I declined, saying I had eaten a late luncheon and would do without another meal. In reality, I was in no mood for talk, and shortly after he had gone, I made my way to the diner, trusting he would not uncover my mendacity.

"I told the steward I had no objections to sitting with others provided they were strangers, so he placed me at a table for four. A gray-haired, florid-faced old man and his comfortable fat wife were two of my companions. The third was a splendid, healthy specimen of young manhood, Scandinavian young manhood, a yellow-haired, sturdy son of Vikings. "The old couple finished their simple repast and left. I was ordering and the handsome young giant was beginning to eat when the beautiful blonde girl I had observed in the sleeper came in and took one of the seats just vacated.

"The girl's eyes and the man's eyes met, and not for the first time, I could see. For their glance was charged with electricity—a bolt of lightning that struck something akin to terror in each. An instant afterwards, the young man was up from the table, laying a ten-dollar note beside his plate, and then he was gone, fleeing from the mysterious horror of this chance encounter with a woman whom God had never intended to inspire young manhood with anything but burning love.

"And the girl, the young woman—I started from my chair, ready to catch her if she swooned. For it seemed she must swoon, so pale she was. But with a marvelous show of courage she forced herself into a state of pseudo-calmness.

"I bolted my meal in a manner that would have caused my doctor intense mental anguish. I asked the waiter for my check and he, observing the young man's money lying there, inquired if I knew whether he was coming back. Before I could speak, the girl uttered a sharp, 'No,' then bit her lip as if in rage that she had said it.

"We were between Harrisburg and Altoona when she appeared again in the sleeper. She stopped beside me and put an unsealed, unaddressed envelope in my hand.

" 'It kills me to do this,' she said in a voice barely audible. 'I am not accustomed to asking favors from a stranger, but it is necessary and you look kind. I am sure you noticed the man, the young man, who was with us in the dining car, who got up and left when I sat down. I think you will find him in the club car and I want you to give him this. I cannot trust it to the porter. Don't wait for a reply. Just give it to him, and then come back here and tell me. Will you?'

"I answered, of course I would, and I begged her to inform me if there was something more I could do. 'No,' she whispered, 'nothing.'

"The young man was easily found. He was in the club car as she had guessed, staring straight ahead of him.

"Without a word I handed him the envelope, and returned to her and reported. She expressed gratitude with a smile that was more heart-rending than tears.

"My instinct, or sense of decency, ordered me not to pry. I took my book to the club car and tried vainly to read, for my brain was consumed with curiosity and anxiety as to what was going on between those two torn souls.

"When at length I turned in, at Pittsburgh, the berth opposite mine was dark and its curtains drawn.

"I rose in the morning as we were rushing through the Indiana town of Plymouth. The curtains across the aisle were open now, but there was no sign of the girl. Nor had she appeared as we slowed up for Englewood. My inquiry of the porter—had he seen her since the preceding night?—was answered in the affirmative. 'Yes, suh. She done leave us three hours ago, at Fort Wayne.'

"I remarked I had thought she was bound for Chicago. 'She sho' was Chicago bound,' said George, 'but young gals, dey got a "unailable" right to change deir min'.' I then asked if he had seen her conversing with a big, blond, handsome young man. 'No, suh. De only man she co'versed to was maself, and ma bes' frien's don't call me handsome or blond, neithuh."

"I waited on the platform in the Union Station and

watched all the passengers as they left the train. The girl was not among them, but the man was, and as he walked out to the taxi stand, I followed him unobtrusively, saw him enter a cab, and heard the starter say, 'Stevens House.' I went to the Sherman and changed, and awaited word from my friend, General Dawes.

"But I could not get my mind off the queer incidents of the trip and you can imagine the shock it gave me to read, in an afternoon paper, the story of a well-dressed, unidentified young woman who had committed suicide by throwing herself in front of the second section of the Broadway Limited at Fort Wayne.

"My duty was clear. I hurried to police headquarters, stated my name, and was received by the Chief. I told him I was sure he could earn the thanks of the Fort Wayne authorities and officials of the railroad by sending one of his men with me to the hotel where I believed my 'friend' of the train was stopping; that if I could find him, I was sure we would be able to learn the unfortunate girl's identity and perhaps the reason for her ghastly deed.

"The Chief delegated Captain Byrne to accompany me. As we drove up to the door of the hotel we saw policemen dispersing a crowd and other policemen lifting from the sidewalk the body of a man, the young Viking, with a bullet wound in his head, a revolver lying near where he had lain, and a newspaper clasped in his left hand.

"There were letters in his pocket, merely business letters, addressed to John Janssen, and the initials on his baggage were J. J. He was the son of one of the richest men in Chicago, and he, the young man now dead, had a wife and children in Lake Forest.

"I know who the girl was, too; the police found her name and her picture in young Janssen's possession. But they didn't tell his family and no one besides a few policemen and myself is aware that there was a girl in the case. The published reason for his act was temporary insanity induced by illness. And if he was sick, I have been dead for twenty years."

Osborne's narrative was over. Dinner was over, too, and Garner and Blades lingered behind the others in the march toward the card room.

"What do you suppose he's got against brunettes?" said Blades.

"And why," said Garner, "do you suppose he won't use the New York Central Lines?"